I0632358

John Veitch

The Tweed

And other Poems

John Veitch

The Tweed
And other Poems

ISBN/EAN: 9783744765688

Printed in Europe, USA, Canada, Australia, Japan

Cover: Foto ©Andreas Hilbeck / pixelio.de

More available books at **www.hansebooks.com**

THE TWEED

AND

OTHER POEMS

BY

JOHN VEITCH, LL.D.

Professor of Logic and Rhetoric in the University of Glasgow

PRISCI CONSCIUS AEVI.

Glasgow

JAMES MACLEHOSE

PUBLISHER TO THE UNIVERSITY

LONDON : MACMILLAN AND CO.

1875

TO

Sir John Murray Naesmyth,

Baronet;

THE REPRESENTATIVE OF THE OLD HOUSE OF POSSO ;

THE DESCENDANT OF THE STILL OLDER HOUSE OF DAWYCK ;

ONE WHO FEELS WHAT IS PUREST AND BEST

IN THE TRADITIONS OF THE TWEED :

These Poems are Dedicated.

CONTENTS.

The Tweed.

Ballads and other Poems.

BOOK FIRST.

Description and Legend.

ARGUMENT.

THE uplands, and solitary spring-head, — Tweed's Well.   Old Wood of Caledon, with Merlin and Kentigern.   The flow and purpose of the stream. Ericstane and Bruce.   Character of scenery.   Tributaries and hills, with their suggestions, historical and legendary associations, from Fruid to Teviot.

THE TWEED.

Description and Legend.

'M ID uplands first to wear the gleam of morn,
  And spread the early sheen of dewy grass,
While sweet wild flowers are breathing odours free,
And clear, air-borne, pathetic bleatings float,
And pewit's cry is heard, half-wail, half-wile,—
Voice dear unto the heart of solitude,—
And heron stalks, then slow majestic sails
Away short space, on low broad flapping wing;—
A lonely well uprises, sacred, clear,

Thine own, historic Tweed, the fount amid
The bent of thy first runlet life of sound.

A treeless wild where pastoral stillness broods,
And but the name,—the Shaws,—memorial keeps
Of sun-unpierced, shape-haunted forest shades,
And birken leaves once quivering in the light
That o'er the grass a dappled splendour shed
In days of other years, ere time and storm
Had swept away the Wood of Caledon.

An ancient wood! dim hanging like a dream
Upon historic memory, wherein,
Before th' ideal eye, quaint forms take life
And as anew embodied pass amid
The greenery of springs revived, the leaves
Of sun-hued autumns, winters dread that swing
Tempestuous 'mid its boughs. The Cymric host
Of storied Arthur bear their ashen spears,

Dim pageantry of battle; rise two shapes,

Weird Merlin and the saintly Kentigern,—

The old bard shadowed by the lurid eve

Of British faith and story,—Kentigern,

The youth, white-robed, yet roseate in the dawn

Of new and holy hope and purer creed.

Gleam on the mantle of the poet seer

Blood-red Druidic signs,—a mantle rent

And torn, as is his noble heart by thought

Of cruel sacrifice, impersonal :

Feeling that will is man within the man,

To make or mar, to be the right or wrong ;

Yet grasping not the great free sacrifice,

The brotherhood of wills. By fountain, stream,

And tree he dwells, as nature-forms of God,

And on the grey stone-circle of the hill,

He sits and eyes the burning sun complete

His daily round ; lone weird communion holds

With spirits of the air, that he may be

The Lord of Nature, may know life and death

And destiny, dread things of years to come;

Beasts of the wood, and birds of air he loves,

Marks Odin's ravens as they circling tell

Of deeds of blood done on the troubled earth,

Scans the great eagle as he dares the sun,

And grim night owls a-hooting 'neath the stars,

For converse high they seem to hold with heaven,

And in their curious eyes he thinks to read

The dark unspoken secret of the world.

Now swept and gone are glade and hazel shaw—

Gone, trackless as the shade of saint and seer,

And 'mid a wild of wilds, 'neath open sky,

All through the summer morn the burnie croons,

In hidden flow, yet flashes oft eye-gleam

From 'neath its brows of slender fringing grass;

And then at night, amid moon-silvered air,

And glory o'er the wide encircling hills,

It pours a deepening sound, continuous,

Upon the calm, as rhythm of the earth

That feels the soothing of the quiet heaven.

A tiny rill of still uncertain fate,

To be perchance soon lost in larger stream,

Or sink unnoticed 'mid the peaty hags,

Like to a broken life that ends in gloom ;

Or, fitting symbol of a perfect lot,

Grow a great river, bear a glorious name,

Reflect to many eyes of short-lived men,

Age after age as they pass o'er the earth,

The high pure lights of God, and flowing flash

Heaven-borrowed splendour throughout all the land.

A streamlet, thou, in latent purpose strong,

A line of force in far south-west that springs,

Aye tending steadfast to the north-east sea,

As thereto moved by phantasy innate,

Or drawn by love of morning's early gleam,

And sun uprising o'er the dappled hills.

But here at distant source who can foresee

A purpose in thy tiny wave, far less

That thou wilt e'er rejoice o'er compassed aim?

Thou'rt as a human life but just awake

To feeling 'mid the world's blank lonely wild,

That gropes all darkly for its fate, and finds

Its end in groping; effort blind becomes

Illumed in act, the life grows free and full

Through striving forces fused: and here, slight rill,

Thou seek'st a way 'mid strong contending streams,

That numerous rush from high confronting glens;

Now nobly is thine impulse full upborne

By loyal south-west flow, and then again

Bent backwards from thy course by north-east burn;

And yet from conflict thou e'er risest strong,

Nay, in thy soft green haughs mak'st gleaming peace.

For there in one fair harmony of flow,

Thou still'st the war of waters from the heights,

And in the reconcilement of the streams,

Grow'st to an ampler life, serener tide,

Till, in accomplished aim, thou glidest grand

In triumph and in tribute to the sea!

The symbol, thou, O Tweed, of those two Lands,

The South and North, that long in conflict strove,

And from their striving found a greater life,

And the strong calm of perfect unity:

Yet wilt thou ne'er forego a pulsing wave,

Deep sympathetic with that noble heart,

The heart of Bruce,—that beat for Scotland's cause,

And made the weaker meet to match the strong—

As now it rests with him of Otterbourne,

Where thou encirclest Melrose' holy shrine.

Thy mountain gleam was in that living heart

To brighten with a hope its young resolve,

Beneath the grey-cloud sky of great emprise,

That morn he rode by Ericstane, his lot

Irrevocably cast for liberty;

And now, if it could beat, 'twould swell to feel

The larger peace, the proud equality,

His spirit through the centuries has wrought

· For his loved land sore stricken ere his time.

Thy lot it is, fair Stream, to flow amid

A varied vale: not mountain height alone,

Nor mere outspreading flat is dully thine,

But wavy lines of hills, high, massive, broad,

That rise and fall, and flowing softly fuse

In haughs of grassy sward, a deep hued green;

No call thou mak'st on dwellers by thy banks

To constant struggle with mere mountain steeps,

Nor leav'st them all to indolence of dreams

On pastoral plain; but, mingling hill and dale

And gleaming pool, like that old Attic land,

Where thought and fancy reached their perfect type,

Thou hast evoked full human energy,

Yet charmed it by sweet breaks of soft repose.

By thee have many lives in quiet passed

Of staid demeanour and of manly mood,

Content with circle of mere homely deeds,

And yet inspirëd deep by breath of song,

That carols now with lark at flush of morn,

Then moves soft-toned, subdued, as hallowed eve

Glows in the west, and dies beyond the hills.

Down many a sky-arched, hill-enfolded glen,

Where summer shadows dwell with mountain sounds,

The speeding stream, uncharmed to rest by birk

That woos it, fair forget-me-not's sweet eyes,

The moss sun-hued, with sparkle as of tears,

The glow of heathery brae, the bracken sheen,

And unarrested by the deep grey rock

That only stirs it to a quicker flow—

Makes haste to greet thee, Tweed, in verdant haugh,

And with its tribute swells thine early wave.

From Birk Craigs grey, far Fruid, pour down thy glen—

The cradle of that knight of Roslin Lee

Whose victor wreath twined round his martyr crown ;

Whose home is now scarce marked by ruined mound,

Time swept, and traceless as his orphans' tears.

Let Hawkshaw come by Porteous' ancient walls,—

Name redolent of noble falconry ;

Haste, Talla, from thy linns and lonesome loch,—

High Gameshope's mist-filled urn,—that shimmering

     lies

Dark grey amid the moors ; speed, rocky stream,

Long uncompanioned, save by hill, and heaven,

And moorbird's wail.   Dread shelter oft thou gav'st

To lonely hearts from men more cruel far

Than nature's cold ; and after rugged flow

Thou circlest to thy close with peaceful wave

Around the mounded graves in lone kirkyard :

The symbol, thou, of those heroic souls,

Unworldly as thy wilds that were their home,—

Their lives as troubled as their death was calm,—

Whom thou did'st keep for God's eternal rest !

Harstane, pour down thy burn from high Broad Law,

The sovran of Tweed's hills ! Great-browed, remote,

Familiar with all winds and wreathing mists;

By winter storm deep scaured; 'neath summer sky

Self-shadowed; throned above encircling heights,

That rise and fall and fuse in myriad lines,

All-motionless, yet, to the scanning eye,

For ever passing on, as wave on wave,

In one far flow, a vast earth-sea of hills,

That ever moves and ever is at rest !

And over all, the quiet of the sky;

The very burns are here deep hid and hushed,

Down far below in long enfolded glens,

Nowhere is man or trace of human hand;

'Twould even seem as if his passing works

Were mere intrusion on Earth's solitude,

Which she but tolerates in paltry nooks,

Where self-inflated he may build and dig,

And come and go and spend his little day;

While here with thee, great Hill, o'er endless heights

Nature beneath that sky rèigns all alone,

Enthroned for ever, and inviolate!

And yet thou keepest well a tender trust

Of simple growths God-given to thy care!

On thy spread slopes peer forms of grasses dwarfed,

Deer-antlered lichen, pale hill violet;

The red-leaved flower, hair-fringed and tipped with dew,

In presence of the sun, as life that keeps

The freshness of its dawn through glare of day;

And here and there a tiny tormentil

That golden gleamed amid the river's haughs,

Now seeking nearer commune with the sun,

Far fearless creeps unto thy loftiest wild,

Companion dear of lonely mountaineer !

Once o'er this high broad Fell the sea-waves broke,

And sea-birds flew and clanged 'mid ocean's roar

And troubled foam; but now at summer noon,

Spirit of solitude ! thou dwellest here,

And brookest not one sound thou canst not fuse

To harmony with stillness; lone stray bleat

That wails the silence, then within it dies;

And ever circling hum that broods at noon

O'er the calm moorland height,—a wandering joy

That makes sweet murmur 'mid the listening air !

'Twas here, O spirit of the mountain lone !

That lives and feels, yet knows no narrow bound

Of rounding space or local consciousness,—

Thou first spake to my heart, and first became

To me a new divine creative power!

I felt how from thine inmost heart there spring

The forms that people all the living realm

Of Poesy impassioned; how we need

A soul in things, and how we're drawn to pierce

Sense symbols of the Earth, and see revealed

To human eye forms on high-ways of God,

That girdle round and consecrate the world!

For on this vast unpeopled wild, alone

With solitude of hills, and infinite

Of void unfeeling sky, I could not brook

The saddening thought of silent self-less things!

I felt the craving deep within the heart

For fellowship of spirit; whereupon

Shapes sudden rose amid the loneliness

To life like mine; above, the clouds sped on,

The sun's fleet messengers, in garb of noon

Arrayed; the sounds of palpitating streams

Grew voices; gentle winds in sympathy

Bent low; and shadows that soft swept the hills

Were ministrants of numerous dim-lit joys.

There was new glory in the sun-cleft mist,

New splendour in the sombre wading moon,

The threat of storm had strange and thrilling
    thoughts:

I felt a Power within the veil of Sense,

That for itself sought outcome meet and true,

Its own expression perfect, its first end,—

Yet e'en for me had sympathetic speech,

If I should lend the ear of Reverence,

Or prize the joy severely-born of Awe!

Erewhile the Spirit pure of God, alone,

Deep brooding o'er the formless dark of things,

Rayed forth the image of his glorious Self,

And lit to God-like life chaotic world;

My faith is that His Spirit still lives here,

B

And communes with the open heart of man
On lonely wilds, where e'er no hand hath touched
The work of God, or marred the holy place
Which he first made a dwelling for Himself!

Where Bertha's form commingles with the mists,
Recalling love and hate, remorse and fear,
That once deep marked the course of human lives,
Now seeming but as shadows on the hill,—
Powmood, foam-dashing o'er thy boulders blenched,
Speed arrow-straight adown thy cloven Hope,
By red scaured mountain wall—name consecrate
To bounding deer and old free forestry;
And Stanhope, 'mid thy rain empurpled breaks
Of stony steeps, pour stream from fivefold springs.
Drummelzier! thou that bear'st the mossy well
And rowan red far up to lonesome hills,
And muirs soft-touched by Merlin's flitting shade,
Come with thy wave in sunshine by his grave,

And murmur 'neath high Tinnies' ruined keep.

Historic streams, ye sweep round ancient homes

That now, alas ! know not their ancient lords !

Impersonal in flow as heedless tide

Of ceaseless Time, and yet so consecrate

By story of the past to names of eld—

To Hunter, Murray, Tweedie, barons gone—

That in ideal presence these still live,

And rule alone amid their burns and glens.

From northern heights, opposing streams, ye speed,

As if on hostile errand, yet are won

To swell Tweed's wave that gleams from bank to
　　brae.

By Chapel Kingledoors,—St. Cuthbert's fane,—

Thou flowest, lonely burn, whose moorland wave

Bore down the glen Lord Fleming's dying wail

As 'neath Drummelzier's brand red-gashed he fell.

How harsh it sounded through that quiet eve

By chapel, where the priest and little flock
Were chanting calm the soothing vesper song !

Dim shade of hart sore pressed, that summer's morn,
Still glooms the brooding pastoral green that rounds
The silver links of sacred Logan Burn,
As it winds gleaming through the Logan Lee—
As pure a stream as pours from mountain spring :
'Twas long ago the seemly hart sped fast,
Before his keen pursuing foes, but still
The shepherd sees him in-the gloamin'-tide,
Has even heard his sad pathetic cry !

Where from the Wormhill speeds the rapid rill,
The sheeted form of that sweet heiress proud,
With light of loving eyes unquenched by death,
Still haunts the Dean ; who wot herself, and well,
A match for young Powmood of olden blood,
But flashed a maiden's scorn on heartless love.

The hurrying suitors' throng, what recked she there?

Or King's swift-riding by the Merecleugh Head,

And lighting at that quaint Mossfennan Yett,

With all his spotted hounds and pomp of chace?

At sunrise in the wood men found a face

Pale, winsome e'en in death;—how there no one

Shall know till God himself arise and flame

His final sunrise searching all the world.

Glenholm, pour gleaming stream by lofty fells,—

And wind around the sacred grassy mounds,

Memorials of the care of olden Church

That loved to dwell among the lonely wilds,

And minister to few and simple folk,—

There set its faith,—Glenkirk and Chapelgill:

Now brooding o'er the past stands high Caerdon,

That fort-crowned watched the homesteads of the vale,

And ready girdled with the bale-fire's glare

The haugh's abodes of peace and piety!

Thou broad-browed Scrape, whom Autumn loves to
    deck
With regal purple crown, thy twin streams bid
Sound down amid thy shadows, through the woods
That circle with their arms the olden home
Of knightly line that ne'er stained knightly name,
But bore the pennon white along the line
Of storied centuries, and laid at last,
In honour down, the well-worn silver shield
Dashed with the sable heads; so fell from fame.
Yet, ancient Dawyck! thy memories alone
Are sweetly sad, for now thou look'st and art
Refined abode of cheerful human ways.
O'er thee a hand has moved with such a grace,
That art, all artless, pure and loving wears,
'Mid sheen of leaf and shade of varied bough,
The simple winning look of Nature's face.

Thy true-souled Knight of olden line has kept

The knightly quality, and this sublimed

Above mere strength, and all that makes rude power,

Has grown and blossomed in aesthetic sense;

And where dark deeds were done on steeps of

    Scrape,

Writ poetry of pine and birken shaw,

And yet has left wild nature free to mix

The heather bloom, pure as the ancient hills,

With spreading boles of stately forestry.

Dark Lyne ! flow sad and slow 'mid dowie haughs ;

Meet thus to pass by Drochil's mouldering walls,—

The symbol of a baffled earthly hope,

And of a broken life uncrowned by fame,—

A home ne'er roofed, or warmed by hearthfire glow,

Or raying forth upon the cheerless night

A kindly light set by a human hand.

Yet strange the glare and troubled does it seem,

That moves within thy desert halls, grey tower,

As years bring round the eve of that grim day

Thy Lord was 'headed on the Castle Hill!

E'en thee, dark Lyne, the Tweed doth smiling greet,

And folding thee within his sparkling wave,

He bears thee onward as a brother loved,

And leaves no stain of thine unpurified!

Flow, Manor, from thy green and sacred urn,

Come with bright heart-gleam through the mist-cleft

    morn

And sundown shade, thou sweetest stream of all

The South! With thee bring memories that float

O'er ruined keeps, and uncompanioned trees

On bare hill-sides, and solitary cairns.

Come in the sanctity that loving broods

O'er those green mounds that mark the ancient shrine

Of sainted Gordian! where the Cross of stone

Points earthwards to the gentle, simple, dead,

And heavenwards rises to the risen Christ!

The mists enshroud it pale, and then it glows

With sunshine fire, robed now in grief, and now

In glory; passing burns together join

Their voices in one ever-flowing hymn;

And yet above it storm wild cries of birds,

As if there were a trouble on the earth:

Lone scene soft-touched by that lone cross, and meet

For meditative thought to stay and brood

Upon the secret tie that binds in one

Th' unworldly spirit living at the heart

Of Nature, and the soul of Sacrifice!

Manor! ere lingering birks bid thee farewell,

And thou art meetly joined with thine own Tweed,

Thou circlest with thy gleam green Cademuir's steeps,

Where murmur of thy streams, and bleatings low,

And many moving shadows of the sky,

Dwell with the pastoral stillness of the hill;

Whose wavy heights keep broken battlements,

And ancient raths now sunk in grassy mounds,

And those weird stones that know no graven mark,

Save grey scaurs written by the storms of years,

Yet silent tell us of long buried dead:

How oft I've felt as there were faces old

Around me, peering dimly from the past,

In grey o' gloamin' 'mid those eerie graves!

Dear hill! of ever changing light and shade,

And faded battle fame in by-gone time,

'Tis thine to charm as thou canst awe the soul.

Let me but speak thee as I've seen thee oft

On a sweet day in early June; o'erhead,

White streaks of wind-slashed clouds calmed on the

     blue;

Around, the hill spring-green, save where the sod

Is pranked with tiny tormentil that loves

The ·mountain slopes, and yellow violets

Of nunlike mien, that groupe themselves afield

In gentle sisterhoods; rock-rose, dear child

Of sun-smote heights, unfolds its fluttering flowers

Of gold beside the heather dark and slow

To greet the sun; in watered hollows green

The slender cardamine, first lilac hued,

Then growing white and pure 'neath influence

Of heaven, a welcome waves to gentle winds

Now vocal with the cuckoo's echoing note.

Frail passing flowers, soft-tinted things of spring,—

Sweet dawn of colour, simple grace of form!

Prelude ye are of richer bolder hues,

Of flowering thyme, the heather-bell and bloom,

And ferns of broad green leafage; yet no charm

Have these like yours, first risen from the grave

Of Winter, when the spirit at your heart

Slept calm, not doubting that in sunny hours

To come, ye'd make a joy on baréd steeps,

Where ceaseless winds were raving day and night,

And all was lone despair; nor any more,

As flows th' unwavering order of the world,

And Autumn draws you back within the veil,

Has that same God-born spirit e'er a dread

Lest ye shall triumph o'er earth's elements,

And live your simple graceful life again,—

Symbols of faith, of innocence, and love,

By doubt unshaken and by fear unpaled!

Great Heights of Hundleshope! that ward the vales

Of Manor and of Tweed, and grandly bar

The southern sky, should ye remain unsung?

Ye that enfold the Alpine glens, wherein

At high noon-tide the shadows lie unscared

In presence of the sun! How many sights

Ye've shown to me! How many thoughts ye've

    stirred

And feelings wrought, since first, in youthful awe,

I eager peered into your far dark halls,

That oped and closed 'mid drapery of mist!

And how I wondered what quaint shapes ye hid,

And what might lie beneath that sky outstretched

Away beyond your tops, so sacred kept

From curious eyes and reach of tiny feet!

Daily I learned your lesson, learned to pause

Within the bounding line that circumscribes

The vision of the soul, and keeps the thought

From wandering aimlessly amid the vague

Indefinite of things, and yet I felt

A haunting power of high uncompassed spheres;

Even when at morn I watched yon beckon slow

Across your brow, the mists, in circling coils,

Sun-smit, transfigured to a dusky sheen,

Then sudden bare your face, and look o'er all

The river vale in splendour of the sky!

Early and long the winter snow enwraps

You in its folds, revealing to the eye

Your sculptured lines, as 'twere the pure abstract

Of nature, bare yet beautiful; and long

A sombre hue ye resolutely wear

Beneath the summer sky, when sister height

Is bright in joyous green, e'en decks herself

With violets amid the glints of spring;

Until the heather through long days of June

Slow changing, unperceived, its russet garb

For robe of tinted green, at length displays

On high a glorious crown of purple bloom,—

A slow won treasure from the summer sun.

How can I speak all I have learned from you,

Ye lonely glens, ye solitary moors?

Haunting your uplands, I have sudden seen

A white mist speeding dusk the summer sky

O'erhead, and fill the depths of glen that fold

The burnheads; and in that abyss far down,

Through the soft veil that hung from all the heights,

In shimmer bright were gleaming silver pools,—

As lustrous jewels parted from a crown,—

That charmed to oneness with their radiant sheen

The drooping fringes of the misty air:

So light of heart, the lowliest on earth,

Doth silently illume and interfuse

With its own purity the dark around !

Invisible powers ye have to stir with dread,

For on your uplands lonesome and remote,

A causeless fear will seize the shepherd's soul,

Even 'mid the stillness of the full noon tide ;

As unseen Pan, in graver mood, of old

Would shadow with an awe lone traveller

On Attic hill, constraining worship from

The simple heart.   But most, when gloamin' grey

Begins to spread its dim and mystic folds,

And things look weird as shades, shades real as

    things,

Will plaided shepherd pass, amid strange dread,

Swift o'er the moorland height, and through the bent,

Until from light of his own nestling cot,

And hearing of his burn, low in the glen,

He snatch a sudden joy, and smile his fear

Away. Nor lonely shepherd only knows

The awesome mood, for oft has poet found

A welcome sight, when after striving miles

Amid your pathless wilds, with cloudy mist

And darkening shapes of gloom, he sudden sees,

Though still afar, the gleam of moon-eyed clock

That high in belfry tower o'erlooks all night

The sleeping town, and ever and anon

Upon the earless darkness clangs the hours !

In the far east I've watched the rising moon

Loom large, a vague rimmed orb of golden light,

That in o'erflow effaced its circling line,

Suffusing in its glow the blue around ;

When up the sky and o'er your heights it passed,

'Twould gather round itself in closer fold

Its floating robes of light, until there grew

Pure brightness set in perfectness of form.

So thus, meseems, does lofty thought progress

To limit and due sphere, for at its rise

Athwart the mind of man, it looms awhile

Indefinite, in unrestrainëd glow,—

A dazzling wonder which we may not bound,—

Full flow of feeling, not idea fixed,—

Then grows to sharper shape and clearer mien,

As sphere enwrapt in its self unity,—

Bright guide across the circle of our night :

Yet as we joy in the pure later light,

Often we fondly backwards turn to think

Of that full glory, weirdly vague and grand,

That thrilled the early vision of the soul,

And stirred and moved us with a dread unrest,

As when the risen light first smote the hills,

c

And ope'd the boundless spaces of the sky !

In moonless nights, full of all mystery

Is the pale weather-gleam that winding flows,

A belt of light above your darkened brows,

And 'neath the hanging blackness of the sky,—

As outskirt of a glory far away,

Dropt faintly on the furthest rim of earth :

And shapes, which fancy to the vision lends,

Appear to come and go on that high-way

Of heaven, shadowy as the forms of those

That were, and now unvoiced communion hold

'Mid the weird gleam, where day and night are met !

Beneath the grey north sky, a quiet stream

Winds a slow wave from uplands bleak and bare,

And 'mid red-earthed, plough-riven knowes that wait

Long time the braird of spring to clothe them boon

In Nature's cheerful green. From Moss of Maw

It comes, that darkly hemmed the painted Pict

In old Manau Gododin, when Modred,

The pagan son of Lothus, striving fierce

With Arthur, they two fell at Camelon.

The British chief, the Saxon thane, the lord

Of Norman name, the vale has known in turn;

Now all are gone, and there is nought the same

As in those days, save, Eddlestone, the flow

And ripple of thy wave among the stones!

Through the old Town thou'st passed in summers

    gone,

In days of gleam, and days of winter storm;

And poured, in calm of night, soft harmony

Round circling wall that fenced the Burgher's homes,

And by the castle that o'erlooked the haughs,—

Now traceless save by mounds of shapeless green.

Dark days of dread, and nights of anxious ward

Men oft have known by thee; thy wave has glowed

With shimmering glare cast from the roofs aflame.

And yet upon thy banks have many lives

Of Burghers old in quiet passed, that felt

The self-respect of daily honest toil,

When none was thought to be a worthy man,

Who bore no badge of useful craft, or guild,

Enrolled a worker for the common weal!

For generations gone thou hast no tear,

All heedless in thy flow; thus thou dost pass

Near an old home, and near a mother's grave,

Whose life was flowering of a noble heart,

To whom self-sacrifice was natural

As is the living breath of heaven's own air.

Her hand was busy as the day was long,

Yet in her eyes the mute appealing look

Of any creature God had made, awoke

Deep sympathy; the harebell on rude bank

Between her fields was to her heart a joy,

And imaged clear in memory I see

The slender waving grass of autumn days,

She plucked, and set above the mantel-piece,

Quaint figured; there all through the winter time

To wear its grace, till living touch of spring

Quickened anew the beauty of the year!

So thou wilt careless pass in years to come

When I am gone, and yet, O simple stream,

Thou shalt not flow unmarked, for all the peace,

And all the love, and all the kindly thoughts,

In days for ever gone, I knew by thee!

Come, gentle Quair, thou dear loved stream of song!

Long consecrate to passion's bootless prayer!

By thee Love's hope has dawned, and dwined, and
    died

Even 'mid the spring, when tender birken boughs

Are growing green, and all the lover's heart

Throbs with upbraiding full, and wild unrest,

That Nature is so kind, and Fate so hard!

And in late Autumn sere, the gentle lamb

Forlorn, sweet orphaned Lucy of the Glen,

When passing from her love, she knew not where,

To the cold world, or not unwelcome grave,—

Heard high on bare-boughed tree the robin chirp

'Farewell'—her own farewell to summer bloom,

And to her heart-stored promise of the year!

And later in these times we've heard a voice

Bid thee, O Quair, run sweet among the flowers,

When love impassioned, in a lowly cot,

Would weary heaven with many a heart-felt prayer,

And blame the blast that blows upon her cheek,

And envious eye the flower that decks her hair!

Come, Leithen, from thy far deep-cloven Hopes

And skyey moors; by White Strath fair and Dale

Of Saxon woe, let Gala Water pour,

And let it glint by Buckholm, Torwoodlee,

As sweet as when it thrilled 'neath his eye-gleam,

That morn the Minstrel, passing to his close,

Smiled softly his last smile on Border stream,—

A smile that played through welcome to farewell!

Let Yarrow speed her flowing wave of song,

And memories braided as of sun and shade;

Glide, Ettrick, from thy Pen and solitudes,

Where croon the grassy rills; and softly sweep

Around the Warlock's stained and mouldering peel,

Where strange lights gleam from midnight unto dawn.

Come, ·pastoral Leader, by weird Rhymer's tower;

Come, South and North, and make an ampler wave

Where lordly Tweed breaks from his mountain land,

To pour his strength upon the Eildon plain,—

Wave meet for royal state of early kings,

Now deep entombed 'neath Roxburgh's smooth green

    mounds;

Meet for hushed clang of hoof and clash of spears,

Quenched foray, and the clear calm moon, unstained

By lurid fires o' night; pathetic peace,

That hovering broods o'er ancient battlefields!

For piety decayed, and holy shrines

To living voice all silent, yet instinct

With quenchless speech of old historic dead.

Here wind, O Tweed, a calm majestic wave,

And glowing gleam in dawn, and glorious flash

In noon, and grandly loom in clouded eve,

In memory of him, thine own in life

And death, who sleeps beside the ancient yews

That changeless shade St. Mary's sacred Aisle!

Eden! flow soft by wooded Mellerstane,

For there the dust of Grisell Baillie lies

Beside the husband whom she loved as life,—

He worthy son of martyred Jerviswood,

She worthy daughter of the patriot Home!

In time of trouble deep none ever bore

A braver heart, or showed a gentler mien,

Than she the lithe lass with the chesnut hair,

And eyes of light and sweetness eloquent,

And ripe rich bloom upon her maiden cheek,

As she would trip o' night to dim-lit vault,

Where 'mid the whitening bones of old forbears

Her father couched, life-hunted in the years

Accursed of bloody Stewart. Oh! at first

Those mounded graves and grey tombstones around

Were eerie to her girlish eyes and heart,

But soon they grew to be familiar friends,

Whose loneliness was welcome, as a sign

That but the unsuspecting dead were near!

With secret message she would gravely ride

To Scotland's Tower, where lay her father's friend,

In prison for the cause of liberty;

With moving shudder deep, and yet with face

Undaunted, she would pass, alone, beneath

The storm-stained heads on grim spiked City Port,

That looked so ghastly in the gleam of morn:

And, mission wisely done, she happy smiled

To see the bonny holms of Merse again !

Yet on her pitying fancy rose the face

Of him, the youth who voluntary shared

His father's cell, and stood by him in death:

Until that face became her light of life,

And seemed unto her heart pure as a star

That shines above the earth in nobler sphere,

Where lives the spirit of self-sacrifice !

The pinch of exile and of poverty

On Holland's shore full bitterly she knew,

Yet o'er the narrow household ways she cast

A sunshine from a soul that conquered fate,—

Full of a peace which nought on earth might

    move,—

To her a strength and to her home a joy,—

And as the well-spring of her noble life

She poured the high refrain, the deathless line

Of song—"Were na' my heart licht I wad dee!"

Fair Teviot come, and join thy spreading wave,

From every glen that cleaves thy storied dale,

Dale of stern deeds, dale of heroic song;

Oft stirred of old by flash of flame, and cry

That 'warned the water,' while the hasty fray

Was borne to every peel, and neither youth

Nor age was backward at a kinsman's call:

As on that night, Bewcastle reiving knew

'Auld Wat o' Harden's' arm, and his stout heart

'That grat for very rage,' when Willie Scott

Upon the ground lay slain; then fiercer swelled,

As, with his good steel cap, the old Laird waved

To onset fresh, while streamed his lyart locks,

White as the snow upon the Dinlay Hill!

Stretch, Teviot, to the Caldcleugh Fell, and stretch

To Caerlanrig, and where the Reid Swire breaks

On English land; come by dark Ruberslaw,

With Jed and Rule, where Thomson's, Leyden's song

Was first inspired by breath of Border glen,

That freshened all our British poesy;

And let thy passing wave by Minto Crag

Now rise, now fall in soft pathetic turn,

To voice the music of that lilt and wail,—

The lilt of lasses ere the dawn of day,

Their sighing at the weary- gloamin' tide,

When all the Forest Flowers were wede away !

Bring gathered flow of all thy classic streams,

And pour with Tweed along the Border line,

A deep full swelling tide, not as of old

Defiant shock of foe, yet strong as then,

And flash a welcome bright to brother-land !

BOOK SECOND.

The Growth of Nature Feeling.

ARGUMENT.

INFLUENCE of the scenery,—river and vale. Nature-feeling in the traditional phrases,—word-pictures,—of the district. Fresh nature-feeling in the early times. Thomas the Rhymer. His ideal. The fairy element. How the early nature-feeling was quenched. The wilder aspects of the scenery. Ossian. Power of reconciliation in the softer aspects of free nature. The first Tweed-side song. Gradual spread thereafter of nature-feeling in the district.

The Growth of Nature Feeling.

BY heritage, pure Tweed, of haugh and hill,
   Which thou possessest with a lordly mien,
From thy high Well to where the ocean tide
Speeds through the arches that two kingdoms bridge,
To greet thine upland wave,—by sunny gleams
Along thy gliding path, by sweep of stream,
And alder-shaded pools,—long hast thou wooed
Thy sons to heart-felt love of earth and heaven.
Silent their love has often been, but deep,
As finding no meet voice, known but to thee,
O noble stream, and those whose hearts were thine !

Chief thou dost teach, by solitude of glens,

And wonders of the sky, the shepherd lad

Who ever haunts thy hills, till in him grows

The deep impassioned heart, and in quaint phrase

He graphic sets both what he sees and feels—

Sometimes in awe, sometimes in stirring love,—

Of daily wonders all around his path,

Not for him wonders, rather daily food,

Unconscious nurture of the inner soul

That gropes amid sense-visions for its God!

'Tis thus at morn he, climbing up the hill,

Has vision of 'the sky' that gleaming grows

Above the east, as fair new risen dream,

Ere brightening orb is seen, or sombre earth,

Beneath, gives one responsive glance; and then

The sun himself appears in radiant glare,

And soft hill clouds pass tremulous morn-smit

In glorious disarray; or slanting beams,

Through watery air, lie 'red upon the rain.'

At high noontide, the vapour floating thin

Before the sun, and o'er the spreading lift,

He marks the darkening 'skaum' upon the sky,—

Till suddenly the whole great light of God

Cleaves the thin veil of air and stands supreme,

Irradiant; while from the height he sees,

Down in the haugh, the creeping shape of mist

Catch the sped beam's far glance, and rise to heaven

Pierced and transfigured, as with fire divine,—

The 'dry ure' glow of sky-enkindled flame.

And many a day above him, on the moor,

The clouds rise high before the speeding wind,

And with them all the fancies of his soul

Take wing, as the grey 'rack' aye steady sweeps

Across the sky, in 'carry' unrestrained,—

An airy fleet, bound on mysterious course,

For ever onwards through the infinite.

'The weather-gaw' he scans above the hill,
Wherein the rainbow's hues with watery sheen
Gleam beautiful upon the grey-dark sky,
Yet ominous of storm; and high in heaven
'The ark of cloud' mysterious gleams and opes,
Then closing sails away into the blue.

And towards day's soft fall, as lowering sun
Shoots slantingly adown the western glens,
And the broad-browed, deep-bosomed forest hills
Lie in their own self-shadowing enwrapt,
That only glooms their green, he reverent feels
The power that lurks in 'scarrow of the hill,'
When strength of mountain and the sound of streams
Are gently folded in the calm of eve,
And all his earth is circled by a peace
That seems to fall as from the throne of God!

Pure joy he has in that deep sweetest time,

The gloamin', when o'er all the face of things

Creeps gentleness, as soothing round of dream ;

The aged man of toil, whose lot is toil

Aye upwards from his youth, and to the close,

Gets from boon nature his one quiet hour

Of rest, and thought, and sober retrospect,—

While in the younger hearts soft passions throb,

And Hope arises 'mid the gentle calm,

And Fancy weaves life-pictures through the years

To come, as placid as that gloamin' tide.

And when the gloamin' shades into 'the mirk,'

There runs along the high hill-tops, below

The darkened sky, above the darkened earth,

A clear pale line of light, 'the weather-gleam,'

In which the day foregoes its ardent look,

And night knows not its unrelievëd shade,

But light and dark are met and reconciled,

Again to part at morn, again to meet

At eve, when each in devious path has filled

Earth's hemisphere, and symboled for our thought

The never-ending outcome and return

Of that great Power that makes, yet is self-grasped

Within the moving cycle of the world.

To dweller in the glen, alone with hill

And sky from day to day, these airy sights

Are beings with a permanence of life,

That seem to come and go undyingly,

As powers that live within the veil of heaven;

Their very names are vital with a sense

Of personality; they people all

His solitude; and thus within him grows

Th' unworldly heart, perchance th' impassioned soul,

And he will fill his vale with voice of song,

Cast upon echo and the wandering winds,

And charming later years in broken notes,

The poet's very name and memory gone.

Where now the Rhymer's verse of early day,

Ere Scotland's life was darkened in its dawn?

Gone from the careless times, yet not unfelt

His spirit lives as glamour of the moon

O'er vale and stream; and in thy murmuring sheen

O' night, fair gliding Tweed, methinks I hear

The distant echo soft of that old strain,

So fairy-weird, which thou hast caught and poured,

Through the long years, in loving memory

Of him who passed mysteriously between

Mid-Earth and Elfland strange, and vision had

Of times to come,—deep-brooding Ercildoune!

A first fresh love was his of nature free,

Of merry morn in May, and dappled shade

Of seemly tree,· by Huntley's banks spring-fair,

And on the Eildons green; while round him rung

The quivering wood with notes of joyous birds,—
The wodewale like a bell the forest through;
And to his ear the mavis mellow-sweet
Aye turned to soft complaining in her song.

Yet in his heart was longing unfulfilled,—
Heart rich with all the wealth of glorious earth,
With all that ear can compass, eye can limn.
Ideals strange, and looming imagery
Of worlds unseen for ever circled round
The margin of his dreams, in sweet unrest :
And as he passed upon the upland moor,
Whereon the noontide glamour shimmering lay,
He felt the silence, come to its last bound,
So absolute in very utterness
That nothing strange it seemed, as suddenly
He caught the sound of huntsmen, viewless far
With echoing horns, one speeding airy blast;
And oft the loneliness of benty lee

Was smote by shapes of knights that moved and
    wheeled,
And flashed upon his 'wildered eye a gleam
Of spears, in direful battles yet unfought
By human hands, upwrapt to all save him
In long dread purpose of the years to come.

Weird, haunting visions these that round him moved,
And awed the soul, left heart all desolate.
But there were spots of beauty sacred, lone,
Pure mosses, quivering birken glades, burn nooks,
Unseen by mortal eye save his alone,—
By passing gleams of sunshine rare illumed,—
Mysterious circles green round heather knowes,
And gentle flowers that waved their airy forms,
When not a breath of earthly wind e'er stirred
Upon the moor. Could these be made in vain?
Had God no creature to enjoy their bliss?
Were there no glorious shapes of beings pure

That floated there in summer noon or night,

And thus redeemed the waste of beauty free?

Such habitations, meet for spirits blest,

Were ne'er left tenantless by Reason, Power,

And Love; and to their beauty, felt within

The human soul, some heart responsive beat.

At length it dawned,—the springtide vision dawned,

'Mid song of birds, and greenery of leaves,—

The dim ideal took clear sensuous form.

She came a wonder radiant as the sun

Upon a summer's morn, the youthful Queen

Of Lower Erd, on palfrey riding fair,—

A dapple grey,—in robe of pearls that gleamed

In their own light; with grewhounds seven in leash,

And by her side seven raches running free.

A silver horn hung dangling from her neck,

Her belt was pendent with barbed arrows keen;

A merry huntress she, so light of heart,

That now she blew her horn, and now she sung ; .

While slender moor-flowers for a moment bowed

Obeisance to the pageant's airy tread.

Graceful she was, with more than mortal grace,

Divine ideal, holy presence seemed.

And he would worship upon bended knee

The sacred face, as 'twere the Queen of Heaven ;

But she forbade the unmeet reverence,

And all unveiled in fairy glamour shone ;

So that he passed from high ideal thought,

And holy mood, and sank upon her love ;

As one whose soul had first been greatly stirred

By opened heaven, and, though to hold it fain,

Is led withal to rest on fair phantasm,

Delusive shape of sense-imagining born.

Thenceforth the Rhymer was mysterious linked

To the weird Vision ; he of mortal mould,

With curious wonder and deep-haunting sense

Of more than mortal fate, passed at her beck

Away from Middle Erd, from sight of sun

And kindly moon, and leaf that grows on tree,

From joy of nature free, through pathways strange

Of awe and terror, 'neath the ancient hills,

'Mid realm of midnight mirk, where shape was none,

And eye could nought discern, but on the ear

There ever broke a roar of rounding sea,

And sough of mighty wave that restless chafed,

In agony, some grim defiant shore,

As beat of surging passion of the world.

At length the darkness and the dread were passed,

And they two lighted in a pleasant land,

Where sunrise never flamed across the sky

In splendour of the dawn, and no bright moon,

Unequal, filled the plains with shadowed light,—

A land that knew no dazzling growth of day,

No darkening fall of night, but gloamin' mild

Perpetual reigned; and all the air was soft

As balmy eve in June; no storm e'er rose

To vex the calm abode; those living there

Had all emotion placid, equable,

No chequered lot, no grief or joy intense,

The calm of pleasure without energy,

That noiseless came as bloom on summer flowers,

And only mildest pains that almost seemed

New pleasures; and there was no death to be

The birth of higher life, or issues dread

And infinite of free will, but all appeared

Fixed state of ended possibility.

They saw a castle on a green-browed hill,

Fairer than any which the sun shone on;

Thither they hied; she blew her horn, and forth

The doors sprung wide, and they two passed within

A lofty spacious hall of roof and walls

Unhewn, as grotto arched and stone embowed.

On either side were rocky pillars high
Of gold and silver, fretted fair with wreaths
Of diamond bright, and nameless precious stones,
Which ne'er had met the gaze of mortal man,
Woven by genii in unfathomed mines,
Bound to the wizard work by fatal spell,
Then cast into abysses that they ne'er
Might simulate the subtle like again.

From lofty roof, by long linked chain of gold,
A hollowed lamp of pearl transparent hung,
And, set within, carbuncle priceless, clear,
That turned to either side by wondrous charm,
And shed o'er all the space mild glowing light,
As that of sundown in an earthly sky,
While back the sparry walls in lustre gleamed.

And all within the hall was pleasaunce gay,
Fair ladies knelt in courtesy before

Their Queen, knights danced by threes, and ladies sat

And sang in rich array,—a motley scene;

And music rare of varied minstrelsy

Arose from lute, and harp, and psaltery,

From gittern, and from airy voices clear,—

Notes sometimes heard upon the moonlit hill,

Weird charm that once may thrill a mortal ear,

But blended here in one grand harmony

Unknown on earth,—now swelling as a wave

That fills the ear, and one lists nought besides;

Then dying as far echo of a sea

In subterranean cave, returning aye

To sink upon itself in ampler mood,

As if it playful touched now birth, now death,

Yet stooped to neither but immortal flowed;

And all who hear are wondering hushed and wrapt

Within the spirit of the viewless sound.

Deep sunk in bliss of sense the Rhymer lay,

The years seemed but a day, until the Queen,

Heart-stirred, bid him pass swift to middle-earth;

For on the sunless sky of Elfinland

She saw a shadow creep, until it grew

A grim dark hand, and knew the coming day

When the foul fiend, each seventh year, has power

To mar the joy, and bear the teind to hell.

But ere he went, he snatched his well-loved harp—

Harp he had won by skill in Elfin song,—

And mingled with its native fairy notes,

Sounds as of streams adown a mountain land,

And strains as 'twere of joyous spring-tide birds,

And voice of earthly love, and sad farewell,

And murmur as of leaves on greenwood tree;

When through the hall there thrilled a piercing wail,

As of a sorrow strange to Elfin land,

Wrung from the heart of burning memory,—

She swooned not as a mortal, but her face

Was wan as water at the winter-tide,—

And all the fairy pageant passed away,

As if it ne'er had been, and Ercildoune

Awoke beneath the greenwood spray alone,

On Huntley banks, save that as on the marge

Of dying dream, he saw a form pass far

O'er benty lee, by distant mountain grey,

And by the falcon crag; while in his hand

He clutched his Fairy Harp that could awake

The memories of that strange land: and since

That hour have echoed through the Border glens

The strains of old romance, and stories dim

Of glamour, gramarye, and wizard spell,—

Of milk-white hart and hind that silent came,

And silent went, and ne'er by mortal eye

Has Rhymer weird been seen on earth again.

Then with him passed for many a year to come

The vision and the power of Nature free.

His fresh-born love was as a gleaming morn

That barely dawned, and then was quenched in gloom

Of long, dark years of mortal strife that came

Fell fast upon the Good King's happy time,

Through one most cursed of cursed aggressive breed,

As if the heaven o'erhead showed what might be

Of beauty for the land, if tyrant lust

Of power had held its merciless rude hand

From blackening all the sky with sickening smoke

Of ruined homes, or left the fresh green earth,

As God had made it, without bloody stain !

How pure the guardian genius of the Stream !—

Of bright and gentle face in summer tide,

In flow robed clear as heaven's own gracious light;

And with a strength that keeps the mastery

Of self, Tweed rushes bold in joy of break,

And then glides on sedate and calm in pool;

Yet often marks the changes of our lot,

For grey-cloud shadows, sudden, throw a veil

Of wavering sadness o'er the water's face;

And, in the gloamin', long wan silent pools

Speak a mysterious sympathy with grief,

As though the stream were widowed of the sun.

And late in Autumn, when the mists have come,

And the dark clouds lie low on all the heights,

And brown decay has seized the wasting leaves,

In troubled flow, O Tweed, thou risest strong,

As 'neath the mighty burden of the skies,

At call of waters hoarse and sounding burns;

Then unrestrained and unimpeded sweep'st,—

By the stern spirit of the hills deep moved,—

To stir the grander pulses of our heart,

And thrill us with the rushing sense of power,

And firmly nerve our souls for high exploits.

On Winter's night, when eye can nought discern

E

Of shape of things, and ear is all alert,
I've heard thee hurrying shout in swoop of flood,—
With voice that rose and fell, and quelled the vale,
As if there surged a people's battle-din.

'Twas this wild aspect awed the early time,—
The outward symból of the deeds it knew,—
Of human passion, fierce as roaring flood;
Men thought of spirits of the air that worked
Behind the veil, that moved in mountain mist,
Tore in the wind, and raged in raving burn,—
Dread literal powers of sense, still unsublimed
By mind, and that poetic thought divine
Which casts out fear, shows terror loveliness.

All save th' inspiréd one,—save Ossian old,
In whose soul dwelt the calm of sympathy
With Nature's sternest voice. He saw and sung
The Tweed, for where Alt-Teutha high and dread,

From rude rock frowned o'er fair Drummelzier's
plain,
Ere deed in Scottish story had been done,
There the bard fought and sung—its lord's hate
sung,
And lonely cave-sequestered orphan youths,
Whose only crime was shedding tender tears,
Amid their father's ruined, grass-grown halls,—
Rebuke that stung to rage the savage heart;
Sung fair Colvala's patient daring love,
Young Colmar's fate, and spectre of the dead,
That, at still midnight, glided o'er the Tweed,—
A brother's ghastly form in moon-lit folds;
Sung deep revenge, when fierce Duntalmo's blood
Dark stained the warrior-poet's burnished spear.

Great bard ! With whom heroic verse enshrined
Thine own heroic deed,—high raised above
The cowering soul of artificial times,

By that full tide of true spontaneous life,

That never dreamt of fear in Nature's face,

But communed with the spirit of the hills,

Soul-grandeur felt in dreaded forms of sense,

In torrent rocks, and deep abyss of glen,

While clear before the poet-seer's eye

Arose strange spheres of things by men unseen,

The wreathing mists, transfigured, passed away

In spirit-shapes sublimed, and all the air

Held mystery of other bordering worlds.

Tweed! most thy gentle spirit loves the smile

Of heaven's own face,—amid the dappled light

Of Spring, when soft white showers, from passing
        clouds

That mottle light the blue of space o'erhead,

First glisten on the green of birken leaves,

And sprinkle all the haughs with twinkling rain;

While, in the sunny blinks between the showers,

The primrose blessing sends from woody braes,

The linnet strains its note to voice the joy

That pulses in the air; the sounding stream

For very gladness gleams; the speckled trout,

Drawn from dark depths of winter pools, disport

In overflow of life and innocence,

And, 'neath the airy insects' sun-bright dance,

Make quiet circlings o'er the spreading face,

Complacent, of the pool with pleasure moved.

For many a day, the Spirit of the Stream

Thus softly spake to eye and heart of man,

Unvoiced, unsung; circled, in breathing Spring,

Around grim towers, where life was watchful, hard,

And heedless of the joy the birds proclaimed;

In summer, spread green haughs and meadows soft

For gentle lowing kine; and flushed the vale

With bloom, the symbol of the year's full strength,

The flower of perfect life; and sought to move

To tender thought, by Autumn's mellow look
On waning birks, that, 'mid the dwining light
Of late October, gently lay aside
Their bravery green, and beautifully die.

But through long years in vain; until, one eve,
The patient, pleading Spirit joyous heard
Its voice re-echoed in melodious song,
From Neidpath's old grey tower, that kept the pass
To Tweeddale's upper glens, and oft had spoke
In other accents to the watchful land,
When from high bartizan the cresset flame
Swung roaring in the midnight air, athwart
Dark canopy of sky, while, far below,
The face of wood and stream, 'mid changeful glare,
Wavering glimmered in a weird amaze.

In that square massive Keep, a child's sweet face
Once made a joy, beneath dim vaulted roof,

Where sunbeam brightness only faltering smote;

And often curious peered through narrow bole,

Entranced by wonder wide of earth and sky.

And him the Spirit of the gentle Tweed

Took for his own fair son, and reared and blessed,

And made him feel and voice his own mixed mood

Of pleasure and of sadness interfused,

The truest to our human life and lot.

For, as he grew a boy, of gentle mien

He was, and sacred in his sight were all

The creatures of the wilds; birds in their nests,

That timorously peeped with shining eye,

Were sacred; their first woodland notes became

His cherished joys; and, towards evening tide,

He loved to watch the circlings of the trout

On quiet pools, and then his deep grey eyes,

As pure and lustrous as a maiden's are,

Yet wearing oft a far clear brooding look,

As seeing things beyond sight's finite sphere,—
Would gleam with gleam of Tweed through softened
    tears.

He sought the streamflow, sought the shining pool;
And when young Passion soared on wing of hope,
Gowdspink and lintwhite's note thrilled through his
    soul,
Made music in his song,—consummate voice
Of joy; but as he knew the changeful mood
Of Love that hovered near, then vanishëd,—
As passing brightness of a sun-smit wing,
That for a moment stoops, and then is gone,—
The mournful cushat's croon, in far lone depths
Of woods, grew dear to him,—dear as a voice
That wails a broken hope; and keenest smart
The exile felt was, that, in distant grave,
His hovering spirit ne'er would soothëd list,
In moonlit night, the Tweed's dear murmuring.

Thus notes of birds and inner music, love,

Transfused in one pure heart, found rhythmic voice,

And struck the key-note of our Tweedside song,—

Joy blent with pathos, native melody;

And, down the years, the strain has echoed long,

Nor echoed merely, touched pure living hearts,

And grown in compass; for with notes of birds

The poet's love has mingled sunny gleam,

And rippling murmur in the soft green haughs,

And all the harmonies of eye and ear,

The lowly flower, the grace of slender birch;

And the poetic soul, once reconciled

Through gentleness of nature to its heart,

Has grown to love bare moor, and lonely glen

Of fear; has felt pathetic power, where man

Is by himself on sky-encompassed wilds;

In pale hill-violet trusted to the winds;

In last brief hum of solitary bee,

By moorland burn, on late September noon,

That dies upon the fading heather-bloom;
Has come to love, with deep-impassioned love,
All simple nature wild, all beauty free
That dwells with innocence and solitude.

Nay, oft 'neath cloud of summer night, strange thrill
He knows, as lone he travels through the vale,
When not a sound is heard from farm or cot,
And no stray light in window cheers his way;
For, ever and anon, 'neath soft warm mist,
That feels the hidden moon, and moveless hangs
O'er silent haughs, and their dark silent trees,
Low river gleams will lapse before his eye,
In silver spaces spread, and stir his heart
To movements that awake mysterious thoughts,
Unknown amid the bright discovered noon.

A kindlier spirit now has grown within
The heart of man,—by Nature part inspired,

And part to Nature given by the soul.

The awesome forest dark is now with love

Illumed ; its shapes and sounds of terror gone ;

Its only sprites the dappled gleams that flee

In thrilling play along the grass, and streak

The shadows of the birk and elm grown old,

E'en win a smile in passing from the pine :

While high o'erhead, between the leafy tops,

The white clouds speed, and, for a moment, gloom

The spaces of the heaven's blue, the eyes

That loving peer upon the lonely glades,

And consecrate the forest solitudes !

Even winter storm, so dread all through the years

Of Scottish story, that it met with nought

Of human sympathy, is now enwrapt

In higher sphere of meditative thought.

The rounding flakes of snow, descending slow

From the bronzed circle of the massëd clouds,—

Once feared as omen of the darkest ill,—

Now teach the soul the gentleness that lives

In heaven's purity. The stormy drift

That wheels upon the air, then pilëd lies

In haugh, and glen, and stills the mountain burn,

Bears fancy high on its fierce rushing wing,

And keeps it wakeful through the roaring night,

Up glens, up hills, and o'er the water-sheds,

Where neither man nor beast may be and live,

Amid the fierce fell tumult of the air.

Yet on the morn when all is still, and o'er

The whitened vale the sun in brightness beams,

The meditative heart has quiet rest,

As if the raging sky and troubled earth

Were, after strife, atoned in one deep calm!

How deep the soul is moved on autumn eve,

When spreading haughs are ripe with golden grain,

And God's rich bounty blesses all the Strath,

To eye the moon, new risen, stay high poised,

Full-globed, on upmost rim of eastern hill,

Whence, for brief space, she loving looks aslant

The westward glen, till its low shadows break

In brightness, through the joy to meet her gaze;

And then, well pleased with greeting of the earth,

Floats calm away to her own silent heaven,

And reigns in full possession of the sky.

BOOK THIRD.

Old Border Life and Poetry.

ARGUMENT.

GRADUAL softening influence of nature-feeling on the life of the old Borderers. Their freedom, courage, impulsiveness. Tenure of estates. Their song and ballad airs. Contrast of past and present. The mouldering Peel Towers. A tradition of Flodden. The Border Muse. Its simplicity, literalness, and fervour. Stirred by heroic deeds, pathos, and supernatural beliefs. Death of Earl Douglas at Otterbourne. Wild nature and the sublime. Modern outcome of old story and free nature-feeling in poetry—Hogg, Leyden, and Scott. Conclusion.

THUS grew and spread amid the flow of years
    The love of what is gentle, sunny, bright,—
A purifying grace that touched rude lives,
And bent rude manners to a finer cast;
For 'twas a troubled time of restless men,
Of daring raids and deadly feuds, exploits
By lee light of the moon, on southern hills;
And these were voiced in thrilling ballad lines,
Direct, intense as passion e'er made verse,
Graphic as truth the heart spontaneous tells;

F

For here, in his lone Peel, the Reiver lived,

And here the Border Minstrel had his home!

But dare we hope, in this self-bounded time,

That any one will for an hour forego

His present world, to feel the shadowy past?

A world it may be wholly consecrate

To famed Utility,—the one-eyed god

Whose culture is divine irreverence!

Perversion of our human nature free!

Yet, think you, can we rise to our true selves,—

Or keep our life harmonious with its type,

If we, devoid of sympathy with power

Of other lives, love not full oft to breathe

The air of old historic reverence?

Then let us lingering pause a moment brief

Upon the dim fast-fading lineaments

Of days of olden story,—catch the look

And soul of those who lived in these grey towers,

Who of a morning saw the sun and sky,

Trod the same haughs and hills, saw river gleam.

And felt the seasons' flow, through centuries

Now gone,—as we, heirs too unconscious all

Of their experience,—not thinking how

The past flows through the present, how the life

We live is tissue woven from the years

That were, by that dread power within the will.

Theirs was a life born of the heaven's pure air,

And nourished into strength by mountain breeze,

By sunshine and by storm; theirs force of arm,

And theirs the courage of long-during breath,

Won from the broad hills they free-breasted trod:

A growth spontaneous as tbe rugged pine,

That, under open sky, unsheltered draws

Its spirit from the blast; and they had hearts

That moved impulsive with the swelling wind,

Among the hills, or through the roaring wood,

Or when it tore and shook their banner stretched

For action bold and daring enterprise.

The sons of men who won them fair estates,

In troubled marge 'twixt English, Scottish rule,—

The trophies of the spear, or purchase free

Of bow and arrow,—won and held from foe

That ever pressed from southwards on their homes.

No marvel that they felt rude power to be

The highest law, and strength the last appeal,

And spurned the feudal claims of all the Kings

In Christenty; themselves deemed rightful Kings,

But not by secondary parchment writ,

By force of arm and custom of the sword.

Thus Outlaw Murray, of the Forest fair,

Kept royal state amid his wide domains,

Where lordly Hanginshaw, from circling woods,

Gleamed rich in blazonry of unicorn,

Of holly green, of knight and lady gay,—

As if the spirit free of forest life

Had overflowed in natural delight,

And easy strength had bloomed in pictured joy.

His treacherous fate on Newark's bloody brae,

At hand of false Buccleuch, the Forest wailed

Through all its glens; as Teviot, Liddesdale,

Long mourned the hard and cruel lot dealt out

To thee, bold laird of bonny Gilnock Hall!

So true in heart they held thee, and so stout

An arm was thine 'gainst dreaded southern foe,—

On that sad morn at Caerlanrig, where long

The withered trees stood leafless, smote by heaven,—

Mute witnesses of passion-prompted wrong!

' By deeds we spread our fame.' ' By might, not art,'—

The mottoes of the time, at length entwined

In one, as those who fearless bore them lie

In one sweet chapel shadowed by the trees,

And gently soothed by ever-murmuring burn,—

Old words that speak of rude forehammer force,

In Border fray, and deadly stroke on helm,

And daring deed on many a bloody field,

Of Edward's wars, of Calais, Halidon,

Of Beauge and Verneuil, of Flodden sad,

And the strown dead that lay from Pinkie's Cleugh,

Face-earthwards, to the gates of Scotland's Tower:

Man was but man as he gave manly blow,

Or, worsted, had the courage of his fate;

Rude power it was, yet let us deem it well,

True strength is that which serves the time's behest.

Yet, when unequal matched with southern foe,

Well could they ply all wily stratagem;

Swift-footed, then they sought their vantage ground

Of hill and quaking moss, found walls in woods,

And from the heights, a lurid rampart dark
Above the flaming plain, startled the night
With shouts of echoing fierceness; thus the foe,
Wildered, and struck by terror high in air,
Fled ere the morn, as if before the sword.

As 'neath the open sky their life grew strong,
So from the breeze they snatched air melody,
That tuned their strength to beauty and to joy;
Sweet sounds they knew of soft pathetic tone,
As simple airs of heaven, spontaneous piped
By pastoral reed,—a wail for absent love,
Low 'mid the broom at eve on Cowdenknowes,
Or deep pure passion's pleading tone in vain,
Beneath the birken 'Bush aboon Traquair;'
And sometimes into low voiced wail 'twould swell
As, born of nightly soughing of the burns,
Or plaintive midnight wind around lone tower,
The note told, o'er and o'er, in lingering strain

The dule of Flodden's dire disastrous day.

Yet prompt their spirits rose, when bugle horn,

Like rush of storm down trumpet-throated glen,

Pealed loud and long the thrilling call to war.

All this old life of centuries is gone,

And we regard it not: new men, new things

Are with us; blood and breed of olden knights

Are rare among us; their bright sun is set,

Their towers are roofless, bare; gaunt, grim walls given

To winds, dank weeds, and-hooting owls by night.

We dread their rule no more, their powers of life

And death, of pit and vaulted donjon-keep;

And children play upon the gallows' mound,

And sit 'neath shadow of the tree of doom.

'Tis well, for 'tis the order of the world;

But 'tis not wholly well, that all should pass

As if it ne'er had been;—true qualities

Of knighthood are true qualities of man :

The truest knight is but the man sublimed.

High courage, honour, prowess, loyal faith

And vassal love they had, if vassal power,—

A bond that sweetly held the hearts of men

Through long descending lines. Oft rapine rude

There was, but it was bold to risk of life ;

No secret coward theft, as ours by stuff

Adulterate, or lying bubble schemes,

That we may lacquer our life's little day.

If busy commerce plied not in our vales,

And means of life were plain and small, we missed

The jarring spindles of a servile strife.

Laird rose 'gainst Laird, but rarely man would strive

Against the master of his love and blood :

Well-knit in cognisance of mutual need.

Shall we not now fuse worldly aim with heart

Of mutual love, that, throwing out the serf,

We yet may truer rise to fullest grip

Of man's right hand in God's own brotherhood!

'Tis well that o'er the present happy look
Of vale and stream, a shadow from the past
Is cast, as of a faded name to call
To mind old history. Oft where the stream
Bends round green knowe, beneath the alder boughs,
There stands the crumbling peel, deserted, lone,
Save for its brotherhood of ancient trees,
Few, straggling, wasted by long tides of storm,
Yet faithful still in their companionship
With relic of the past, the broken home,
Left by the careless years to sure decay.

Think,   once   in   these   old   towers   what   feelings
        wrought,—
There bridal joy, and children's sunny smiles,
A mother's hopes and fears, a father's cares,
And all strong thrillings of this life have been,—

Home-welcome flashed to victor from old wars,

Dead burden borne from fatal feud o' night;

Ay such that 'tis a marvel this dull earth

Should lie so callous 'neath the memories,

Unless it be that surely in its breast

It keeps them latent for the final morn.

There, where the mounds rise green o'er ancient
    home,

And all is silence save the ceaseless dash

Of passing waters o'er the whitened stones,—

There, was a sweet wife's clinging parting sad,

When husband 'bodin' in the feir of war,'

Boune for dire Flodden's reckless chivalry,

Rode forth a gleaming wonder to young eyes

That eager peered from height of bartizan.

Long dread suspense there was, long hoped return,

And then dim sough of that disastrous day,

That passed, ill-omen'd, through the shuddering land!

But him his vassals' love bore, faithful, back
From hated southern field, from strangers' earth,
That he might lie beside his kindred dead;
O'er moss and moor, and o'er brown mountain ways,
They wended with their burden, shoulder-borne.

At sun-down, resting in a valley low,
They saw, between them and the western sky,
A solitary tower, grey, roofless, rise,
Where once a powerful lord had ruled the land;
A darkening mass, but through a narrow bole
High near the top, there gleamed a ray serene,
As cast from heaven beyond; and, lingering there,
The day slow dwined to shade, thus passed and died,
A strange, weird way of death on that tower-top,
That moved and thrilled in hearts of all these men
The waiting spirits of old memories!
Then sadly looked they on their own mailed dead,
And thought of all the prowess of his house,

And of the fair slight maidens orphaned there.

And on they wended through the moonlit night,

'Neath shadows of the crags, as passing palls

That softly touched the rigid, armoured form

They bore aloft; by mountain burns they went,

That poured sad requiem, now paused, now moaned;

Till, as the robins waked the Autumn morn,

They reached his own grey tower, and passed within

The iron gate; and, 'neath the vaulted roof

Of däis hall, they laid him down,—where oft

He princely sat,—his piercëd hauberk on,

His visor down; on moveless shoulder spread

The silver shield that bore the sable heads:

Now, utmost feat of loyal duty done,

When o'er him widow sobbed and children wailed,

Sprung the first tears of those stern loving men.

Slow passing forth there was from that grey house,

And in the grave beside the dead was laid

Joy of one living heart, and that fresh mound

Seemed in a widow's eye earth's dearest thing.

Yet now, nor mound, nor stone is found to mark

His resting-place, and tower slow follows tomb,

Till house of life and house of death alike,

Beyond all memory gone, are smoothly dressed

In folds of summer grass, where dull sheep browse,

And shepherds, heedless, tread upon the fame,

The nameless fame, that lived in other days.

Can we once marvel, that, with deeds like these,

The Muse that broods amid the hills was stirred

To verse heroic, tender, human, true,—

And oft heart-fired by strains of old romance?

Unknown to fame she was, nor heeded phrase

Conventional that charmed a worldly crowd

That never felt the simple modes of life,

And never looked pure Nature in the face;

As Queen she ruled within the Border Land,

In Teviot's uplands wild; 'mid lonely glens

Where Ettrick creeps; by Yarrow's pure green holms,

That pleased and silent list the lively strain,

As loch-born waters leap from calm to sound,

And joyous flash by many a bonny knowe;

Yet gather sadness towards evening tide,

As gloamin' shadows o'er the Dowie Dens.

She spoke from simple heart to simple faith

And fervour, with a voice as of the scul

Of acts that thrilled the time; a pure response

It was, no hue of personal colour blent,

Or trick of art, or ornament save what

Unconscious flashed upon the narrative,

Austere, of pictured deeds, yet marred it not:

The shallow stream doth mingle with the scene

It shows its own poor pebbles; nobler lake

In eyes of calm and depth profound has power

To mirror for us every feature fair
Of the o'ershadowing earth and sky it feels,
In purest picturing; its sparkle clear
But lights, not breaks, the perfect imagery.

Of waiting, reverent mood, a Muse content,
If she could but be true to what she saw
And felt of deed heroic, bold emprise,
Rough hardy ways of life, inspired throughout
By natural impulse, pity for the fate
Of him who fell, unequal matched with law:
High chivalry she sung, and feudal faith,
And simple pathos, and bright humour's gleam
Upon grim acts, as sunshine lights grey crag:
Love's dawn of hope, and its too tragic eve
'Mid moonlit flash of spears, at shadowed stream;
And passion's agony, in twilight gloom,
Of that lone maiden, with her lips all red,
From kiss on kiss of her dead lover's wounds!

And, rounding all, the quaint weird shapes that girt

The world of sense, and ever and anon,

Would sudden flash upon our human life,

To stir by fairy form of elf, or awe

By moving wraith, distinct, of living man !

Yes ! to these times of ours this faith hath power !

Not faith, but vision ! In low cottage lies

The dying man ; his wife with him alone

'Mid lonely moor ; one passes to them there

On eerie road at evening fall, with heart

Of hope and tenderness, and memory

All wakeful, stirring in her mind the things

Of by-gone years. Then sudden on the brae,

White with the stubble of the gathered corn,

She sees him stand, the sick man silent stand ;

Yet fair and strong as e'er he passed in youth,

His staff in hand, his plaid o'er shoulder thrown,—

As he and she, when neighbours, joyous walked

G

From far farm town, together to the Fair.

Soul-awed she knows the dire presage, and yet

She eager looks, without fear looks upon

The vision, as, with face turned to her face,

He slowly westwards passes calm away

Into the dim vast night, yet 'tis as morn

About him, all encompassed strange with light !

And then there lies nought but the dark grey sky,

Above the misty rim of wavy hills ;

And when she gains his cottage, he is dead !

Oft sprite wails drear in waters ; often shriek,

That passes swift o'er dark hillside before

The keen pursuing storm, is heard as voice

Of shepherd's doom prophetic ; for, as morn

Breaks dimly red upon the calm that fell

Where the wild storm all through the night had
        been,

And purples with faint streaks the snowy hill,—

'There lone he lies, the young life stilled and hushed,

White palled beneath the gleaming drifted wreath,

Wrapt in his plaid, his duty grandly dared,

Self-sacrifice complete; the peace of God

On his pure fearless face that, mid the dark,

Has seen the light of an unearthly dawn!

This Muse would speak, in eerie dream o' night,

To stalwart man, who ne'er in battle blenched,

And though, all through the stricken field, he bore

Within his heart the weird presage, knew not

The nerveless arm; but, when his wound was deep,

The dying knight, in ghastly grey of day,

Still bid his friend keep heart, for he had seen,

In boding dream, a dead man win a field,

And knew full well the dead face was his own!

All through the moonlit night to break of day,

The wave of battle gleamed, and heaven's pure peace

Was strangely mingled with the fierce onslaught,

The cries, the pallor, bloody agonies

Of dying men; and now the silent moon

Is fading in the west, and every face

Of eager Scot is ruddy with the flame

Cast from the rising morn; they sweep the field;

But he has softly passed to other dawn

Than that now breaking over earth and sea!

Yes! lay him—'tis his prayer—by bracken bush,—

The stricken knight whose dead face won the field!

And let the bent wave withered in the wind,

With mournful grace of fair dishevelled hair;

Let moorland breeze make lonely requiem,

And sky-grey clouds shed soft drops on the scene;

Then bear him, loving hearts, on plaited bier,

In his stained armour, to the altar's pale

'Neath holy roof, where lie belovëd dead,—

There nightly voice a yearning for his soul,—

Meet sanctity for him of Otterbourne !

And oh ! the maid had sore heart on the morn,

When, through the night, in vision on the braes

She, with her love, had pulled the heather green,—

Weird of her hope snatched ere it reached its bloom.

The mother mourned, if e'er her bonnie bairn,

Whom she had happed so kindly in his bed,

Came sudden at the hour of mirk midnight

Upon her visioned sleep, the green birk round

His brow,—the sacred tree,—for thus she knew

That he would soon be girt in Paradise !

Wild nature well she knew,—this simple Muse,—

And felt its sway, sometimes a fear, again

A thrilling awe as of power undefined,

Thus dimly growing to a purer sense

Of things sublime; and yet aye bold to face

And dare the utmost might of storm and flood,

The haggy moorland dark, and lonely tracks

O'er benty uplands through grey gloomy night;

Feeling the will within us higher still

Than Nature at its most, and grander far

Than all the dim vast powers 'gainst which it strives,

E'en when it stricken fails and is o'ercome.

Dark was that eve when the strong swell of Clyde

Roared loud and louder on the lover's ear;

Ne'er swerved he, man or steed, but swam the stream,

His one quest to the flood, 'Make me your wreck

As I come back, but spare me as I go!'

A Muse too restless, and too close engirt

By weird and wild, to feel the depth of power

That woos to love of gentle Nature free;

Yet this pure love was working in her soul,

For oft she spoke to fervid shepherd lone,

As, in sweet summer-time, he passed along

The green hill-side, the soughing burn below,—

Spoke in sky-visions, and in sounds of air,—

The strange low voice of spirit of the moor,

As yearning of a soul, deep, unfulfilled,

Mingled with hum of bees on heather-bells;

And with her gracious face so near she stooped

Before the 'wildered, dreaming shepherd's eyes,

That he would secret bear, within his heart,

New feeling of a presence deep and pure,

Yet know not how to give it outward form,

While, through its power, unconsciously he grew

In simple manners, and in reverent mind.

At length, within a herd's house lone and low,

Down by the burnside, in a cloven glen,

Where afternoon came soon and morn rose late,

Set far beyond the haunts of living men,

On skirts of solitude and desert fear;

As, on a winter's eve, the peat fire glow

Cast o'er the wall quaint-flickering light and shade,

And, from the dark outside, there fitful came
The windy swing of storm-tried, bare-boughed ash,—
The cot's one tree,—a keen-eyed mother crooned
To eager listening, sympathetic son,
The stirring strains of the sequestered Muse.

He, Ettrick's fair-haired Shepherd, Nature's child,
Thus knew weird forms that girt his daily round,
Soared vision-wrapped 'mid high unearthly realms,
Lord of the world of awesome imagery.
Yet he would weave around unearthly scenes
A grace that binds them to our human heart:
Ideal form, incarnate to the sense,
That ne'er had met the gaze of living men,
Rose at his touch; the light of sinless land
Shone in her eyes, when fair Kilmeny came,
Once back to Earth, amid the gloamin' peace.

The sanctity of Ettrick's mountains green

Was o'er his youth, and, shepherd lad, he knew

The grandeur and the loneliness that dwell

Amid the shadows cast from Black-House Heights,

Where even summer noon has tinge of awe;

And yet a tender hue is on the birk

Down in the cleugh, on sacred nook of green

Low by the burn, and gentle thoughts are born

Of intermitting sough of mountain streams:

There Loveliness with moorland Pathos dwells

To soothe the heart of Solitude and Fear.

'Twas thus he grew to living sympathy

With what is tender, pure, in daily sights

And sounds about his path, from morn till eve,—

When lark soars skyward, till "the Kye comes

    hame!"—

He loved the bleat of lambs amid the spring,

The lowly primrose in sequester'd glade,

The daisy that outspreads 'its silver star,

Unheeded, by the mountain burn'; and dear
Was vision of the 'dappled vales of heaven,'
With mountain-side and tree, at evening fall,
Upon the Loch's calm breast, that slept and dreame
A quiet gloamin' dream of earth and sky !
Yet strange things all, and stern to him wer
    joys,—
The moving cloud that visored broad Clockmore,
When Cramalt, gathering all her rainy springs,
Poured wild and wayward from her skyey Crag,
Not heeding grassy nook or heather brae,
Where she had lingered through the summer time.
He loved, as only poet's heart can love,
The flashing levin and the winter storm,
And Yarrow's flooded roar, and sounds dim heard
Of airy tumult 'mid the driving mist.

So Leyden caught and poured impassioned strain,–
Whose ardent spirit rose with soaring wing

Of hooded erne that rode the rack, high, dim,

Onsweeping through the sky, 'where Ruberslaw

Conceives the mountain storm;' a broken life

Was his, alas! with promise unfulfilled:

A man 'mong men, who rose to what he was,

In pure outcome of free spontaneous power

His God had given; and o'er his early bier

Two Muses met,—the Muse of Scottish Song,

The Muse of Eastern lore,—to mourn him dead,

To wail their broken hopes, but yet to joy

That he had kept his dearest trust, his prayer,—

Th' unselfish heart, the innocence of youth!

And He, the king amid the minstrel band,

Witched by the mountain Muse's bridal ring,

Wooed and won the coy shape in her retreat,

Displayed her glorious to admiring eyes,

Enriched with greater far than natural dower;

And Time has sealed espousal meet between

The Minstrel and his loved romantic bride.

Smailholm ! bare, grey, crag-rooted Border Keep,

Stern as the storms and as the deeds thou'st known,

An old deserted home ; o'er hall and hearth

A silence lies as of long buried dead !

The Spirit of the Past from thee first charmed

With awe the lonely brooding infant's heart,

By visored faces grim that on him peered

Through rusty window bars; yet here and there,

Amid thy rocky braes, thou had'st in store

Soft spreading tufts of loveliest velvet green,

And wall-flower sweeter for its ruined home,

To win his love for gentle Nature free !

And when above thy tall, quaint form, grim Keep,

The sky grew dark in folds of thunder-cloud,

Lit by the levin flash, the wondering child

On green sward dauntless lay, look heavenward fixed,

While his poetic soul grew bold to snatch

A strange and weird delight from Terror's heart,

And eye with fine stern joy the face of Fear!

Sweet Ashestiel! that peers 'mid woody braes,

And lists the ripple of Glenkinnon's rill,—

Fair girdled by Tweed's ampler gleaming wave,—

His well-loved home of early happy days,

Ere noon of Fame, and ere dark Ruin's eve,

When life lay unrevealed, with hopeful thrill

Of all that might be in the reach of powers,

Whose very flow was a continued joy,—

Strong-rushing as the dawn, and fresh and fair

In outcome as that morning of the world,

Which gilded all his kindled fancy's dream!

A dream of old Romance,—of Love and Faith,

Of Honour, Valour, gentle Courtesy,

All natural to life as daily deeds,—

As simple impulse felt and straightway done,

While no one, wondering, thought the noble strange !

Weird tales and legends floated in the glens,

Like broken shapes of mist that come and go

Athwart the wavering dawn of summer morn,

To pass with it and be like it forgot,—

Until his time,—the latest Minstrel's time,—

When they transfigured rose on high in shapes

Of glory, many hued, before the world,

Sun-smit, by Fancy's mighty orb of fire,

That beamed from Heaven across the hills of day !

The Past is now before us with the power

Of living presence ; Minstrel, thou hast charmed

Oblivion of its prey, called living form

From many a mouldering grave, made ruined home

And lone hill-cairn, and mountain stream and glen,

Instinct with voice as real as speaks to sense,—

Made Scotland, conscious of her chequered life,

Thus know herself,—her glory and her shame !

Let us be stronger for the ancient deeds,

Let us be purer for the ancient crimes !

And let us keep and prize the Minstrel's love

Of Nature free, and manly human soul !

The love that breathed all through his moving tale,

And quickened all the age,—let this be ours;

'Twill freshen wearied heart and jaded life,

Reviving as the morning breeze that blows

From holms of Yarrow and from heights of Tweed !

How clear thy ripple, Tweed, this dewy morn,

As clear as if thou now rejoicing sprung,

At thy first birth, from confines of the hills,

And all the myriad years were still to come

Of storm and sunshine, troubled sounds and floods,

That yet have moved all traceless o'er thy face !.

Art thou the same through those long chequer'd years ?

Immortal 'mid the mortal lives of men !

As ever-gleaming truth 'mid passing shows !

Or dost thou die each eve amid the gloom,

When slow I see thee fade and pass away,

Thou and the Sun,—and both are born afresh,

With each new morn, new-births God-purified?

To me nor Sun nor Stream has tinge of eld.

Thou, River, but the white and aimless mists

Upon the hills, each morn by God's own hand

Upgathered calm to one pure flowing life;

Thou, Sun, each morn new made, the orbëd sum

Of the vague glow and scattered fires of dawn,—

River and Sun, the symbols of a Hand

That opes and shuts each day upon the world,—

Both old as Death and yet as young as Youth !

Ballads and other Poems.

H

SIR SIMON DE FRESEL, Frasel, or Friselle, and later Sir Simon Fraser, Lord or Laird *(Dominus)* of Oliver Castle in Tweeddale, was the most notable man in the middle period of the War of Independence. His father was the head of a house, ancient and eminent, as early even as the time of Alexander III., and was one of the *Barones* of the kingdom, who took a prominent part in the settlement of the Scottish crown after the death of the Maiden of Norway. When the design of Edward I. to usurp the superiority of the kingdom became obvious, the son stood by the national side. Fraser was present at the battle fought near the Castle of Dunbar in April, 1296, when the heroic Countess, sinking the feelings of the wife in those of the patriot, gallantly held the castle against both her husband and the lieutenant of the English King. Perhaps the news of Edward's red-

handed sack of Berwick, a few days before, had some-
thing to do with this unwifely but womanlike resolution.
The Scottish army, or rather assemblage of men, was
badly beaten by the Earl of Surrey.   Among other
persons of note, Sir Simon Fraser was taken, and sent
to an English prison.   He and a neighbouring laird,
Simon de Horsbroc, got back their liberty and lands by
doing fealty to Edward, and serving with him in his
expedition to Flanders in 1296-7.

After this, Fraser was for some years in the English
service in Scotland.   His patrimonial estates, lying
chiefly in Upper Tweeddale, comprised Fruid, Oliver,
Drummelzier, and Neidpath.   He was thus appropriately
made Edward's Warden, or Governor, of the Forest.   The
office, indeed, had been in his family under the Scottish
kings.   In this position his loyalty to the English King was
at least once suspected by the Governor of Edinburgh
Castle, John de Kingston, but nothing came of the surmise.
We find him engaged in several important matters in the
service of Edward, down to the siege of Caerlaverock in
June, 1300—when his sable pennon starred with six silver
"rosettes"—not roses proper, but the cinquefoil strawberry flowers—appeared amid the splendid pageantry of
England on the shores of the Solway.   The following
year, however, September, 1301, Fraser had cast off his

allegiance to Edward. Risking life, estates, and throwing away his prospect of high advancement under the English King, he, in the autumn of that year, joined the band of patriotic Scots under the Earl of Buchan (Comyn) and Sir John de Soulis, who had risen in defence of their old established monarchy and national liberties. They were now harassing the English garrisons of the south of Scotland ; Buchan and Soulis with their men are lying at Loudon ; Sir Simon Fraser is in command at Stanhouses. On the 10th September, Soulis attacked Lochmaben Castle, and after doing some damage withdrew his forces.

The fortunes of the Scottish party were now at about their lowest ; nearly all that was left them was their unconquerable spirit. Yet, it was at this period that Sir Simon Fraser, impelled almost certainly by a patriotic motive, and knowing well what he had to expect from the inflexible and persistent hate of Edward, revolted from the English interest, and cast in his lot with his country's cause. He was a prominent leader in the irregular warfare which annoyed the English garrisons and so greatly exasperated the English King. At length Fraser and Sir John Comyn of Badenoch, got together a body of troops, chiefly from the Forest, and the dales of the Tweed and the Clyde, large enough to attack the English on the open field. They marched quickly through the night, across country, from the uplands of the Clyde or the Tweed, and in the grey of a February morning in 1302-3, surprised the English forces, separated into three divisions, on Roslin Muir, and gave them a severe defeat. The Scots did nothing so marked against the southern occupiers of the country until Bannockburn. The victory of Roslin Muir was not in itself of signal importance, yet it helped to cheer the somewhat drooping spirits of the Scots in their very unequal contest with the armies of Edward. The popular rising in which Fraser was a leader was in a great measure repressed by the English towards the beginning of 1304. There was then a capitulation of the staff of leaders who had professed to rule Scotland in the name of King John—particularly the Guardian Comyn and his party. Edward, now feeling that his policy of violence, terrorism and blood had done nothing to reconcile the people of Scotland to his rule, tried his hand at a turn, unusual for him, of what might be called clemency. Comyn and his followers gave themselves up, and were received into "the King's peace," under a stipulation for their lives, liberties, and lands. To Fraser, Soulis, and others were proffered life and lands as terms of submission, with the additional proviso of banishment for limited periods. From any saving clause, however, of capitulation, one man was always held excluded—William Wallace—the type incarnate to Edward of the popular opposition to his will, and the heart hatred of his feudal temper. Highly to the credit of Sir Simon Fraser, he, territorial lord as he was, declined Edward's terms of life and lands so long as his friend Wallace was not included in the clemency. In a Parliament or Convention held at St. Andrews, composed partly of Scottish Barons, in the spring of 1304, the garrison of Stirling, Wallace and Fraser were declared outlaws. After all the other Scottish leaders had sub-mitted, Wallace and Fraser are acting together more closely than ever, and still waging the unequal fight. As late as March, 1304, they are found standing almost single-handed against the English lords, Latymer, Segrave, and de Clifford, at Hopperowe — obviously Happrew — on Fraser's estate in Tweeddale. Then we hear of them in "parts of Lothian." It was not until after the capture and barbarous death of Wallace, 23rd August of next year, that Fraser submitted to the English terms—safety of life and temporary exile. He was ad-mitted to these terms in the Parliament of Westminster, 13th October, 1305, some three weeks after the execution of Wallace.

When Robert Bruce, the grandson of the Bruce of Baliol's time, set up his standard in 1306, Sir Simon Fraser was ready to join him. He was present with

Bruce at the skirmish at Methven, when he is said to have three times saved the fallen King, heavy in armour, from being taken prisoner, by setting him on his horse. What he did for the King, however, he was unable to do for himself. He was among the notable captives of the skirmish, or he was taken shortly afterwards. Barbour quaintly puts their fates thus :—

> "Sum thai ransownyt, some thai slew,
>   And sum thai hangyt, and sum thai drew."
>
>   *The Bruce,* ii, 272.

Fraser was too tempting food for Edward's sweet revenge, to escape the last-mentioned fate or fates. He was sent to London, and there, in the spring of 1306-7, underwent the barbarous and worse than brutal doom, usually accorded to those who had frustrated the imperious will of the King. A decent veil is thrown over the details of his end in the following succinct account of it, given by Leland from the *Flores Historiarum :—*

"Anno D. 1306.   Pugna inter Robertum *Pseudoregem* Scotiæ, et Almericum de Valentia comitem Pembrochiæ, prope Methfen in Scotia.

"Simon Frisel, antesignanus Scotorum captus, et Londini postea tractus ac suspensus."

There is one touching incident honourable to human nature which ought to be recorded. As Sir Simon Fraser went to the gallows, and as he stood under the gallows tree, his fine personal appearance and his noble bearing—worthy of the man who preferred patriotism to life and worldly honour, and of the baron who had been the last to leave the grip of the hand of Wallace—drew expressions of sympathy not only from the tender hearts of women, but from the prejudiced and less susceptible men of the rough London mob, who crowded round the scaffold to witness the last and horrible agonies of the captured Scot.

The Earl of Athole, of the old line, suffered along with Fraser. Edward was ill at the time, but the news of the capture and execution of the Scottish patriots served to revive his languishing spirits.

Sir Simon Fraser left two daughters, co-heiresses. Mary, the elder, married Sir Gilbert Hay of Loch-quharret, afterwards Locherwort, and now Borthwick, an estate lying near Catcune, not far from the head of the Heriot Water. Borthwick Castle was built on the moat of Locherwort. Hay was a man thoroughly imbued with the spirit of his father-in-law,—a spirit probably inherited by the daughter; otherwise he might not have been her choice. He did eminent service to Robert Bruce. He was a party to a bond, in 1308, that obliged him to defend the cause of Bruce against, in its quaint language, " all mortals, French, English, and Scotch." He received with his wife the large Tweeddale estates. These were for several hundreds of years held by his not unworthy descendants, the Hays of Yester—a stock now represented by the Marquis of Tweéddale.

The other daughter married Sir Patrick Fleming, said to be Sheriff of Peebles, to whom came, either by this marriage or by inheritance, the Barony of Biggar. Sir Malcolm Fleming, the elder brother of Sir Patrick, was made Earl of Wigton in 1342. This branch of the family became extinct, the last of the line having sold the estate and earldom of Wigton to Archibald Douglas. Eventually Fleming of Biggar was made Lord Fleming, and then Earl of Wigton. The Biggar family continued to represent the old lines of the Flemings and Frasers for several hundred years. It is now merged in that of the Lords Elphinston. Like the Tweeddales, the Flemings quartered the Fraser arms—the strawberry flowers. Their motto was, *"Let the deed shaw."* The story that Sir Simon Fraser left a son, who founded the Lovat and Saltoun families, is, I am persuaded, a mere myth. If the Frasers of the north sprung at all from the old stock of Oliver and Neidpath, it was from a collateral branch, of which there were many. Possibly they descend from Simon Fraser, the son of Sir Andrew Fraser, Sheriff of Stirling, the uncle of Sir Simon, the hero of Roslin. This cousin, Simon Fraser, true to the spirit of his race, fell nobly fighting at Halidon Hill in 1333. The Lovat and other estates in the north may have been first acquired by a son of the Oliver family at a considerably earlier period ; but the first Fraser designated of Lovat is Hugh in 1367. Neither Lovat nor Saltoun descends lineally from Sir Simon Fraser.

WERE I NOT STIRRED BY SCOTLAND'S OLDEN BLISS,
NOT FOR EARTH'S EMPIRE WOULD I BEAR ALL THIS.

The Lord of Oliver and Neidpath.

I.

SCOTLAND IN THE TIME OF EDWARD I.

WILD glen of Fruid, and Oliver
    Set on the rocky steep,
High Tinnies, massive Neidpath grey,
Quaint relics of a long gone day,—
    What memories ye keep !

With you back runs our thought beyond
    Queen Mary's hapless morn ;
And Flodden's dule by sluggish Till,—
The darkest day of Scotland's ill,—
    And peerless Otterbourne :

When the calm moon from heavenly height
  Leant down with gentle face,
Saw fierce strife rage beneath her light,
Yet spread o'er helm of outstretched knight
  A weird unearthly grace !

'Yond luckless hill of Halidon,
  And sacred Bannockburn,
That dim and light with shade and gleam
Old Scottish story's moving stream,
  Through many a chequered turn.

Back to that February morn,
  When hearted as the free,
The patriot lord of Neidpath poured,
With flashing spear and gleam of sword,
  Tweed's sons on Roslin Lee.

The Southern King, hard-purposed, stern,

   Had stretched a ruthless hand,

Beyond the Cheviots' barrier high

To Maidens' Tower against the sky,

   And grasped the Scottish land!

" From South to North one kingdom all,

   Until the restless sea,

That sounds my power from shores of Gaul,

Shall bear my name 'mid wild birds' call,

   Round storm-girt Orcady.

" I who have awed fierce Saracen,

   The pride of France laid low,—

Shall I be baulked by rude Scotsmen,

Rough peasants of the mountain glen,

   Disloyal rabble foe?"

Three leopards on his banner shone,
　Of fine gold set in red,—
In aspect haughty, fierce, and fast,
Unfeeling as the biting blast,
　On cruel purpose sped.

'Twas fate of men both true and good,
　To feel the savage rage;
And ladies high of royal blood
Knew well the beast's ferocious mood,
　Each barred in iron cage.

By Wallace, Seaton, Nigel Bruce,
　The slakeless thirst was fed,
And oft in simple hamlet lay
A gory sight to shame the day,
　And none to earth the dead!

Fierce through the prostrate land he passed,

   Burnt village, town, and farm ;

The lead from old church roof he tore,

Spared covering o'er the altar floor,

   Too pious it to harm !

Much recked he flag of mild St. John,

   From Beverley's old Fane,

That aye 'fore English host had shone

When Scotland's soil was trampled on,

   Since days of Athelstane !

God help the land, was many a prayer,

   From heaven-bannered host !

Caerlaverock's fate proclaimed the truth,—

As for the weak he had no ruth,—

   The brave he hated most !

I

With hirelings base the land was filled,
  Who knew no law but will;
All lived in shade of tyrant fear,
No man was safe, knight, churl, or peer,
  Nor wife, nor maid, from ill.

Each pleasant thing, horse, hawk, or hound,
  That gave a simple joy,
Or sweetness lent life's daily round,
Some base pretext was ready found
  To seize or to destroy.

Thus long the looming shadow lay
  Dark on the saddened time;
The memory of the Good King's day,
When there were gamyn, glee, and play,
  Fell like regretful chime.

Ah ! tinselled Lord, puissant, cold,

    Why recked ye not your plan

Of mere mechanic sway and mould

Is death of kingship, treason bold

    To sacred cause of man?

While the white flower of sovereign power

    Blooms fair, spontaneous, free,

In sun or gloom unchangëd still;

The outcome of a people's will,

    Heart growth of loyalty !

Oft rode through Neidpath's court-yard door,

    A knight of Norman name ;

Strawberry flower on shield he bore,

What was a lowly bloom before,

    Uplifted into fame !

Of ancient line he came, yet knew
　　Lot chequered as a dream;
Had seen our Scottish story's morn,
Had watched its darkened noon forlorn,
　　As cloud glooms sunny stream.

He fought beside Dunbar's sea-Keep,
　　When one noble lady, bold,
Stood firm against proud Edward's power,
'Gainst King and husband held the tower,
　　As stout as Earl of old!

For she had heard the rumour dire
　　Of Berwick's bloody morn;
A wife, but yet a woman more;—
That mother's face gashed in its gore,
　　And her gashed child new born,

That lay upon the Berwick brae,

   Beneath the open sky,

Had waked the pathos of her heart,

Had stirred her to a stern, strong part,—

   'Twere better far to die !

Fraser was ta'en by that old tower,

   To English prison sent ;

Where Flemish fields were red with blood,

By Edward's side unwilling stood,

   To Edward's fealty bent !

Lord of the Forest now he roamed,

   All life to him was fair,

He need but quench his noble heart,

He need but take the baser part,—

   That hath no cross to bear !

"My oath! But do I bear a bond?
I've sworn but to his might;
I've bartered 'gainst my country's weal
My life, estate,—ignoble seal,—
Prized Self above the Right!

"What get I by my oath but this,—
I shall ignobly be?
What if the law of sacrifice
Now calls me above self to rise,
That this poor land be free?

"Life cycles in the years that pass,
And richer fruit they bring;—
I, what am I, 'mid passing cries?
And does not every leaf that dies
But make a fuller spring?"

From moorland chase, with trophies strung,

   Of glancing spear and bow;

'Mid wondering looks of vassal band,

Who did his hest with ready hand,

   He rode, desponding, low.

Wrapt in his thoughts he communed still :—

   "Is all this strength of arm

The blood of simple deer to spill?

For creatures straying wild, this will

   To do them deadly harm?

"All purposeless this life I lead,

   Outlet of impulse blind,

Mere aimless energy of deed,

No guiding end or noble need,

   More than the passing wind;

"Or rushing burn that leaps the fall,
  And joyous fills its pool;
Yet there are weak to aid, and call
Of injured to redress, and all
  The land knows cruel rule.

"The winter wind I've known it tear
  And rave across the lee,
All through the spring, and ruthless bear
The benty locks of lint white hair
  As spray upon the sea.

"Seemed windy sweep the power supreme,
  Yet lowly on the earth,
Unwatched a grassy blade would gleam,
Down in the nook of mountain stream,
  The new time's sacred birth:

" So in my heart I seem to feel
  Young purpose silent grow,
Spring-omen of my country's weal,
To English tyrant forced to kneel,
  'Neath wasting storm laid low.

" If slight as growth 'neath withering wind,
  Yet from the mute dull earth
That yearns for life, I lesson find—
That mere brute force long cannot bind
  The soul that feels its worth."

In action prompt, in friendship true,
  In wary counsel learned;
The burgher's hearts unto him grew,
The muirmen of the forest through
  All to him longed and yearned.

Not fearing peril, life, estate,
  Heart-touched by public wrong,
At length he cast his lot and fate
Against proud Edward's power, and hate
  Deep, unrelenting, strong.

II.

THE RISING AND BATTLE OF ROSLIN.

The need-fires flamed all through the night,
  Flamed red from peel to hill,
Brave hearts leapt up with sense of might,
And gentle women feared the sight,
  As bode of looming ill.

The burghers wakeful eyed the glare
  That beamed across the town;
The river caught the ruddy flare,
And bore it through the dark night air
  By cot and farm adown.

Hauberk and helm they donned at call,

   Grasped pike clear, keen, and long;

And soon within grey Neidpath's hall

Surged murmuring storm, one heart in all,

   Of unavengëd wrong.

Ere greyking of the misty morn,

   With Fraser on the lee

Four knights, his peers, in fealty sworn

To aid their country's cause forlorn,

   Rode, famed in chevachée.

Horsbroc was there of Saxon line,

   And there, in blue and gold,

On Burnet's helmet shone the vine,

Strange to our heather-hills the sign,

   Of richer clime it told.

And there too Posso's laird,—the Bard,—
Of sweet poetic name;
His song, where crags the falcons guard,
And still his line keeps royal ward,
Now lost to fickle fame.

And Vache of Dawyck there, who yields
In stout bold heart to none;
Yet fancy decks him sunny fields,
And, Vascon vine-slopes flushing, gilds
With morns of days long gone.

Now his Scrape's mist-filled mountain urns,
And for Garonne's still gleam,
He hears the murmur of the burns,
He sees Tweed move in rippling turns,
As in sweet chequered dream.

A patriot passion moves his frame,

  A glowing warmth of blood—

Unto young Scotia's cause he brings

A soul that, crushed, undaunted springs,

  More keen, the more withstood.

Through long dark years, on many a field,

  The pennon of his line,

When brave hearts death or victory sealed,

Waved white, and gleamed the silver shield

  Dashed with the sable kine.

Last, Hunter of Powmood, who strung

  The arrow speeding free,—

Name consecrate to bounding deer,

To joyous chace o'er moorland clear,

  And noble forestry.

Ne'er spurned he couch by mist deep drenched,
  Far from the haunts of men,
Where his wild burn from springs unquenched,
Leaps breaking through the boulders blenched,
  Adown its skyey glen.

Ah! wild it raves in winter time,
  And dread its waters' war;
When summer streaks the mosses green,
It courses bright in sunny sheen,
  Beneath the stern red scaur.

Silent they move through Meldon pass,
  Where misty morn was spread;
On the Black Hill, ere break of day,
Rose sudden red a flickering ray,
  By sacred fire outshed.

Hearts quickened by the omen good,

    They passed hag, burn, and scaur,

Passed through dim pastoral solitude,

Where cot and farm in quiet stood,

    To dire dread shock of war.

And here and there, through lone peel bole,

    Peered mothers', maidens' eyes,

Who crossed themselves, and prayed, and blessed,

As line on line still onwards pressed—

    Sons', lovers' bold emprise.

From uplands of the southern hills

    They shot on Roslin Lee ;

As sudden shape from out the mist,

As levin from the dark cloud pressed,

    Came flashing fell and free !

Not long the shock, nor long the rush
  In onset on the plain ;—
Of mingling spears a shivering frusch,
Of unreined steeds a maddening crush,
  That trampled fallen men :

Whose corslets pierced shed drops of life
  Upon the red-wet grass ;
And then with sway of sword o'erhead,
The muirmen, wave unbroken, sped
  Against the bending mass,

That quailed and surged amid strange cries,
  Prayer mutterings on the ground,
Hoof-ring on helm, and painëd groans,
Faint signings of the cross, weird tones
  Of death's low moaning sound !

But late on Falkirk's bloody field,

   Within the spear line's sheen,

The Forest bowmen low were laid,

The tallest and most graceful dead,

   That Southron foes had seen!

And 'twas their sons now forward pressed,

   Men of the muir and fell,

Fair-haired, keen-eyed, warm-blooded they,

And think you they forgot the day,

   They'd heard their mothers tell?

The patriot force resistless spurn

   New bands, one after one,

That for dear honour ardent burn

The forceful tide of war to turn,

   Twice ere the set of sun.

K

Then, triple victory gained, avenged
In blood of fallen foe,—
With savage hand, stroke ruthless, sore,
The heavy load their country bore
Of unredeemëd woe.

That gloamin' to their mountain homes
The patriot band repair,
But with their joy some soft tears blend,
As by a moorland tower they wend,
And lay their burden there.

At morn as by the peel they passed
A noble widowed dame
Gave fair haired son, true-hearted, leal,
An offering for her country's weal,
The last hope of her name!

At even-tide her arms she throws

    The pale young form around,

Less tearful than at morning hour,

Though now she knows the shadow's power,

    Since he had nobly found,

In the last battle's shuddering shock,

    Of the fight's varying flow,

The place of triumph and of death,

'Mid turmoil thick and panting breath

    Of hated foreign foe !

Ah ! Roslin Lee, but glint of sun,

    By cloudy sky o'ercast,

And yet ye cheered a nation's heart,

And nerved it to a trustful part,

    Till freedom dawned at last !

By moss and muir, by loch and burn,
   The Lord of Neidpath lay,
And still he waged the unequal fight,
Spurned policy, and feared not might,
   Through many a bitter day.

And when o' night his camp-fire gleamed
   By secret hag or scaur,
The Forest folk would eye the sight,
And inward bless the lonely light,
   Their hope's last glimmering star !

Comyn and Soulis ! Let them take
   The terms of tyrant's grace ;
No truce with English King will he,—
Nor life, estate, nor liberty,—
   Where Wallace hath no place !

Wallace ! the type of Scotland's will,

   Edward's incarnate hate !

His last grip of a brother's hand

Was Fraser's by Tweed's silver strand,

   Ere he passed to his fate !

Now years have gone, strife's ebb and flow,

   And 'twas the time when high

On our hill-tops the winter snow

Is smote by April sunshine glow,

   Through blue breaks of the sky.

Brown moss spots peer amid the white,

   And streaks of tender green ;

And shapes of mist, before the sight,

Rise up in wreaths, and quaintly dight

   The grey rough crags of whin ;

Then skyward move, and softly part
  In incense to the sun;
Each burn with fresh found voice takes heart,
In joy of new-born force alert,
  And shouts as it doth run.

While bleatings all around are rife
  Of lambs amid the spring;
The patriot knight, 'mid bursting life,
They bore far south from child and wife,
  In grace of graceless king.

As the braird shot, as bud took bloom,
  And Tweed flowed peaceful down,—
Ah! Nature recks not our heart's gloom,—
He calmly passed through traitor's doom,
  To wear the martyr's crown!

Oft from dead sire to son hath flowed
   One great undying aim ;
'Twas a slight maiden orphaned now,
In whose blue eyes 'neath sunny brow
   There gleamed the father's flame !

From where amid high Borthwick's wilds
   Lies field of old Catcun,—
He came, Loquharret's knight, the Hay,
His country's and the Bruce's stay,
   And Neidpath's heiress won !

For six dark years great oath he kept
   To stand by Bruce's side ;
He, noble Seaton, and Lochowe,
Three banded to the death in vow ;
   So bid Loquharret's bride !

'Till that June day the Southron knew

Power of a dead man's hand;

When tyrant's son rode fast and far

From Bannockburn to old Dunbar,

No more to lord the land!

The Hart of Mossfennan.

They hunted it up, they hunted it doun,
They hunted it in by Mossfennan toun,
And aye they gie'd it another turn,
Round by the links of the Logan Burn.

OLD BALLAD.

'NEATH Powmood Craig the hart was born,

And thence in the dawn of a summer morn,

By startled mother's side as it lay,

'Twas brought by a youth for his sweetheart's play.

She was a blue-eyed maiden fair,

Of stately mien and flaxen hair,

The daughter meet of an olden race,

Remote as a flower in a moorland place,

That blooms to all the great world lost,
And yet once seen is prized the most,—
Pure wood nymph she of Caledon,
Who loved all creatures wild and lone.

The gift to her was priceless, dear,
Since the giver, laid on a plaited bier,
Was borne away from a far off field,
With a spotless name, with a blood-stained shield.

To her of an eve the creature bent,
While to him a simple grace she lent,
As she comely wreathed his noble head,
And decked his brow with the heather red.
Fond she gazed on those lustrous eyes
That met her look with a sweet surprise
At a face so tender, sad, and fair;
She thought they read her soul's despair;
And through her frame strange thrill would go,

As she caught the chequer'd pass and flow

Of trembling motions in their great deeps,

As light and shade o'er the mountain-steeps.

Far o'er the moors on a summer day

H'ed pass and roam and freely stray;

But ever, as shade of evening fell,

He turned to the home he loved so well.

His heart yearned aye to the lonely wild,

While his love was that of a human child,—

That set a bound to his nature free,—

For the maiden's face on Mossfennan Lee.

The hunters are out this summer morn,

They sweep the moors by hag and burn,

By rock and crag, each high resort,

For dear they love their noble sport.

They started a fee at Stanhope Head,

And down the glen the raches sped,

Fire-flauchts lanced up from each horse's side,

For the galling spur was prompt to chide.

Round he ran by Hopcarton Stell,

The spotted hounds pressed on him fell;

I' the haugh he took the Tweed at the wide,

Then tossed his horns on Mossfennan side.

Still the cruel hounds are on his track,

In his ear the yell of the hurrying pack,

Fain to Mossfennan Tower he would turn,

But the chace is hot,—to the hill by the burn.

They hunted him high, they hunted him low,

They hunted him up by the mossy flow;

The lee-long day, from early morn,

The Hopes rung loud with bouts of the horn.

No bloom of heather brae them stayed,

No birk-tree quiver or sheen of glade,

No touch of nature` bent their will,

In hot blood onward, onward still.

Powmood, that ever in clear or mist,

In fray or hunt the foremost pressed,

Now speeding keen as north-west wind,

Late i' the day left all behind ;

Save Dreva's Laird, ne'er boding good,

Wide was he famed for a reiver rude,—

And hand that took kindly aye to blood,—

Left blacken'd walls where the homestead stood.

They hunted the hart these two alone,

Till the shadows lay in the afternoon ;

Where brae was stey and bank was steep,

The noble fee fell in a gallant leap.

They blew the mort on the Wormhill Head,

Where sore he sighed and then lay dead !

Oh ! why not let the creature be,

Bear his noble head o'er hill and lee,—

That ate but the wild roots, drank o' the spring,

And roamed the moor a seemly thing,—

Joyed in the sun, flashed fleet in the storm,

Free in the grace of his God-given form !

The merry sport of the day is o'er ;

I' the gloamin' at the old tower door,

No gentle creature is there to greet

Her eyes that seek him, sad and sweet,—

Oh ! with love's last link 'tis sore to part,

And feel but the void of the aching heart !

The merry sport of the day is o'er ;

Rose the creature's sigh its God before ?

Hearts harder growing through breach of ruth,

I ween this is eternal truth :

That gloamin', after words of strife,

Saw Powmood's blood on Dreva's knife !

The Death of Lord Maxwell

THE Battle of Dryfe Sands was a crucial fight. The Maxwells and the Johnstons had long striven on the Borders. There had been hot blood and bated breath for some years; but now the pent-up passions of the clans were to find outlet. The Laird of Johnston, through his maternal relatives, the Scotts of Eskdale and Teviotdale, had received a body of 500 men headed by Sir Gideon Murray of Elibank. Lord Maxwell, the ninth Baron, proceeded as Warden of the Marches to meet the Johnstons. He had in foot and horse 1,500 men, while the Laird of Johnston, with the Scotts and Murrays, reached 800, or thereby.

On the 7th December, 1593, the two forces met on the Dryfe Sands, near the Solway. Lord Maxwell, trusting too much to his superiority of numbers, and not considering sufficiently the advantage of position of the Johnstons, risked a battle, and suffered a sharp defeat. Before the battle, a reward had been proffered by Maxwell for the hand or head of Johnston ; and Johnston, hearing this, in turn readily proclaimed a reward for the hand or head of Maxwell. In the rout of the Maxwells, Lord Maxwell, "a tall man and heavy in armour, was in the chase over- taken and stricken from his horse." After this, he was either slain by Johnston of Kirkhill or left wounded with his hand cut off,—for which the reward had been offered. The tradition to which the following ballad refers is that the wife of James Johnston of Kirkton Tower had gone out to look for her husband and relatives, who were engaged in the fight, and having come upon Lord Max- well lying wounded, despatched him as here related. (See Mr. Fraser's *Book of Caerlaverock*, I., 29.) I may add that I first learned the story of the death of Lord Max- well, as here given, at least twelve years ago, on one of those quiet evenings which hallow my memories of the cultured homes that surrounded the ancient University of St. Andrews. The following ballad was written long before the *Book of Caerlaverock* was printed.

The Death of Lord Maxwell

THE Leddy sat alane i' the Peel,
　　A' through the weary noon;
For the fray was struck at early morn,
　　And now the sun was doon.

Nocht she saw of the fecht that swung
　　In deid grips frae the tower;
But distant soughs would rise and fall
　　Of mortal strife and stour.

L

And hurrying birds, ane after ane,
  Fled seawards frae the land,
And every shriek that crossed the roof
  Was a wail from far Dryfe's strand.

"I'll oot and see how fare my sons,
  I can thole na' this unrest"—
She locked the door o' the auld grey keep,—
  Wi' the airn key hied her west.

She hadna gaen a mile, a mile,
  A mile but barely one,
When there she saw a deid man's face,
  I wot, 'twas her son John.

Nae stop she made but further sped,
  And by the Red Syke fa',
There streakit lay her lad Willie,
  The flower among them a'.

"A curse upon the Lord Maxwell,
  An' a curse upon his name,—
'Tis he has wrought me a' this dule,—
  God wyte him wi' the blame!"

The evening tide was warstling sair,
  Sair warstling wi' the faem,
Aye bearing straight upon the sands,
  Deep moaning as it came.

But whatna wounded man is this,
  That lies upon the strand?
I wot it is the Lord Maxwell,
  And they've hacked off his hand!

"Oh! Leddy Johnston gie to me
  Ae cup o' water clear,
Unhook the basnet frae my heid,
  I'm faint for want o' air."

"Now by my sooth ye fause fell loon,
  Sair Lord ye've been to me,
'To set her hood' ye brunt Lochwood,
  My sons lie deid by thee!

"Nae cup o' water shall ye get,
  Nor yet a breath o' air,
But a reft mother's hate ye'll ken,
  Ere lang as ye lie there."

She gae ae look to the western sky,
  It frowned a lurid red;
She didna turn that way again,
  For a fear was overhead.

Ae moment's grip o' the tower door key,
  She swung it ower his bree;
They fand the great Lord Maxwell cauld,
  Next morning by the sea!

The Lady Fleming's Dream.

JOHN, the second Lord Fleming, Great Chamberlain of Scotland, Ambassador to France,—the representative of one of the most energetic and distinguished families in Scottish military and civil history,—was assassinated, while hawking, by James Tweedie, the son and heir of John Tweedie of Drummelzier, on the 1st November, 1524. The scene of the deed was on that part of Lord Fleming's estate which lay in the uplands between the Biggar Water and the Tweed,—the highest reaches of which are Culter Fell and Caerdon. He was accompanied only by his son and heir, Malcolm, and a few servants. The Tweedies lay in wait for him on the moors with a considerable body of retainers. The ground of quarrel was the ward and marriage of Catherine Frizzel (Fraser), the heiress of Fruid. Drummelzier laid claim to the feudal fine and wardship, and James Tweedie, son of

Drummelzier, wished to marry her; while Lord Fleming, on the other hand, sought to secure her for his (canonically) illegitimate son Malcolm.   When the parties met on the moor, hot words ensued, and young Tweedie drew his sword and killed Lord Fleming on the spot. The Tweedies robbed the defenceless servants, and carried the young Lord Fleming to their castle of Drummelzier Place, where they confined him.   Legal proceedings connected with the murder went on for nearly seven years; but, after all, such was the weakness of law in the minority of James V., that the banded assassins escaped with a mere pecuniary payment.   They seem to have been well backed, if not instigated, by Sir Walter Scott of Branxholme.

Lord Fleming had rather a varied and not very creditable matrimonial experience. He first married Euphemia Drummond, daughter of Lord Drummond. A dark suspicion attached to him that he poisoned her and her two sisters.   He then carried off Margaret Stewart, daughter of the second Earl of Lennox, whom he afterwards repudiated on the ground of propinquity in blood, and lack of previous dispensation.   His third wife, Agnes Somerville, of the house of Carnwath, survived him.

The Lady Fleming's Dream.

" FARE ye not with the hawk this morn,
   Fare not, my lord, my life,
I've striven last night with a fearsome dream
   Long hours of eerie strife!

" I saw o'er the ridge of the Culter Fell
   From the south a darkness creep,
Shapeless and slow it moved in the air,
   Some purpose dread in its keep!

" Down the Culter Hope it moved and swung
  Till it wreathed itself to form,
And there it grew to a black bull's head,
  With a threat as of gathering storm.

" And then 'twixt me and the new risen sun,
  It darkening poised i' the air,
'Twas vain I strove the light to see
  For the horror hanging there !

" Face to my face the grim thing kept,
  And over Boghall Tower,
Instead of the blink of the morning light,
  'Twas dark at the morning hour !

" And yet methought 'twas not by might
  That it quenched the sun of day,
But watchful aye it moved and turned,
  As wile seeks noble prey !

" From the lift at last the grim head passed,

And lo ! the clear moon shone,

Yet I marvelled why she stood in the sky,

When I looked for the morning sun !

" On a hazel glade her beams were shed,

In a hollow deep of the fell;

Soft and bright was her sparkle light

On the face of the Hunter's Well.

" And near it, methought, I saw a form

That knelt to the water fair,

And went and came as in trouble deep

For some one lying there !

" In the Well she bathed a new-cropt flower,

It seemed the strawberry pale,

Sadly she eyed its drooping face,

As in grief without avail !

"I knew the lady's face and form,
    She lies in the sun-dark tomb,
But once she sat your well loved bride
    In power of her youthful bloom !

"The Fleming wears the strawberry flower !
    My lord, my life, take heed !
Drummelzier bears the black bull's head,
    Dark omen ye may read !"

Lord Fleming's look was startled, strange,
    Yet he mounted his horse and rode :—
"I'll fare with the hawk this winter morn,
    Recking nought night fancies' bode !"

But as he passed o'er the moorland fell,
    Low words he muttering said,—
Seemed as he spake to some one there,
    "Is there ruth ev'n with my dead ?"

He thought him of a clay-cold form

   That lay in a chapel girth,

He marvell'd if but the loved in heaven

   Keep watch o'er the left on earth !

High they coursed o'er the spreading fells,

   Till late in the afternoon,

And far they rode by the lone burnheads,

   Till up i' the east shot the moon !

Below from the Hope there seemed to come

   As 'twere a dim cloud gleam ;

Is this but the mist of the water-side

   Struck bright by the glinting beam ?

Out of that mist there sudden flashed,

   A young face keen as flame ;

Scant words but hot between them passed ;

   They bandied a lady's name !

One stealthy thrust from Drummelzier's sword,
  And then a deep-drawn wail;
The strawberry white on the Fleming's breast
  Grew red in the moonlight pale.

Dead he lay by the Hunter's Well,
  Dead horse and hawk by his side;
Drummelzier and ten arméd men
  Rode late that eventide!

They rode by Chapel Kingledoors,
  With clattering hoof they sped;
And well the priest in the lee moonlight
  Knew omen of their tread!

All night on the moor Lord Fleming lay,
  Face to the moonshine clear;
Next morn to Boghall they brought him slow
  From the hill on a sauchen bier!

His lady deemed him fair that morn,

   When they brought him from the heath,

Soft pallor on his upturned face,—

   'Twas hard to think it death !

Pale and fair as his strawberry flower,

   New snatched with drooping head;

For aye cut off from its quickening root,

   Yet a grace is on it dead !

The Herd's Wife.

IN a lone Herd's house, far up i' the Hope,
 By the hill with the winter cairn,
She paced the floor i' the peat-fire glow,
 In her arms she clasped her bairn!

Out in the night, the snow-storm's might
 Tore wild around the door;
"Oh! waes me for my ain gudeman,
 Up on that weary moor!

"I canna bide that gruesome sough,
  And swirl of blindin' drift;
There's no a star in a' the sky,
  Nor a glint o' moon i' the lift !

"Has the crook o' my lot then come sae soon
  On our gleesome wedding-day?
Wi' the ae bloom o' the heather braes
  Is my blessing sped away?

"Oh ! bonnie a' through was our year,
  Frae Spring to the Lammas-tide;
There was joy in the e'e blinks o' morn,
  Was I wrang in wishin' 'twad bide?

"But little thocht I that the hay,
  Deep ower the haugh and the lee,—
Our first crop he sae blythely mawed,—
  Was the last we thegether wad see !

" Have I loved him ower muckle, O Lord,
   Thocht mair o' his smile than Thine?
Oh ! on earth I had nane but himsel'—
   To be my sweet bairnie's and mine ! "

She paced up and down, the bairn in her grip,
   That knew not her sore unrest;
And aye about it her arms she clasped,
   Pressed it, how close, to her breast !

High on the blast rose a piteous whine;
   She thrilled as 'tween hope and fear,
'Twas the pleading wail of faithful Help,
   But alone,—no Master there !

No warm hearth seeks the old dog to-night,—
   His face is set to the storm,—
He's come from where his master lies,—
   He'll guide to the snow-numbed form !

One tender look has the wife for Help,

    A tear-eyed glance for her child;

Out will she 'mid the fearsome night,

    For him that lies on the wild.

With milk in vial, her sole resource,—

    Laid in the warmth of her breast,—

She and Help 'gainst the 'wildering snow,

    To her God she leaves the rest!

Fearless she faced the gruesome sough,

    And swirl of blindin' drift,

There was no a star in a' the sky,

    Or a glint o' moon i' the lift!

Bareheaded slept he 'neath the mound,

    Where the wreath was o'er him laid,

There in the folds of the winding snow,

    Help found him wrapt in his plaid!

M

Oh! how she clasped him there, and poured

Life-warmth through the chillëd frame,

Heaven tender looked on her wifely love,

He breathed and blessed her name!

Peden's Grave.

THE prophet-preacher was first laid in the Churchyard of Auchinleck, in the Laird's aisle. After six weeks his body was taken up, and thence carried or dragged by a party of dragoons to the place of public execution on a hill near the adjoining village of Cumnock, where it was re-interred "out of contempt." The following is the inscription on his tomb in Cumnock Churchyard :—

"Here lies Mr. Alexander Peden, Faithful Minister of the Gospel, some time at Glenluce, who departed this mortal life the 26th of January, 1686 : and was raised after six weeks out of the grawf and buried here out of contempt. Memento Mori."

The people of Cumnock, who had formerly buried in the churchyard round the church, in the hollow where the village stands, abandoned their ancient burial place, and formed a new one on the Gallows Hill, enclosing in it Peden's grave. Within the rails that surround the preacher's tomb lie the remains of the Covenanters David Dun and Simon Paterson, who were both shot on the spot where they are buried. Two hawthorn trees grow above the graves.

Peden's Grave.

LONG were his troubles, and watchings o' night,
   Wrestlings till grey o' the morn;
At last from death-couch on the moor,
   To the kirkyard tenderly borne.

By Lugar side low he was laid,
   Lovingly happed with the sod;
From earth they asked nought but a grave,
   His spirit at rest with his God!

But out of God's acre hate tore him,
    Out of the sacred kirkyard,
No rest there for God's own elect,
    The place of crime his award!

Through Lugar's deep woods he was borne;
    Birds hushed their carolling,
As onwards the ghastly shudder crept,—
    Dead face through the leafy spring!

They have dragged him on up the brae,
    To a hole 'neath the Gallows Tree;
There to lie and rot in contempt,—
    I' the place of shame aye to be!

Yes! wreak your poor hate on the corpse,
    No doubt the work's to your will!
The soul's might is too high for your scope,
    Or the martyr spirit to still!

Ye ne'er scrupled to quench a man's life,

Or hack the corpse with the sword !

No more would have spared the dead Christ,

The face of the Crucified Lord !

Think you, have you power o'er the man,

Who degrade the mortal form?

Are ye deaf to a people's murmuring,

That swells to the sweep of a storm?

Cavaliers, forsooth ! Cavaliers !

Proud in your mindless might !

For order, for law, for the King?

How stand you there in God's sight?

Can we hope hearts like yours will e'er learn

That conscience and freedom are things

Which in union make noblest law,

Whence alone true order springs?

Think ! no more in the old graveyard
   Will any one bury his dead !
They carry them high to the Gallows Hill,
   And lay them there at his head !

Love seals with the silence of death,
   Where hate sought to blast his name;
Hearts are drawn to the saint lifted up,
   Christlike in the glory of shame !

Mute Nature e'en yearns o'er the spot,
   Earth and heaven their off'rings bring,
The hawthorn grows green o'er his sod,
   It blesses with sweet blossoming !

Tasso. 1596.

EACH heart was touched
When through the fair Italian towns there passed
That tall majestic one, with face so pale,
And eyes all lustre, and a look so strange,
As if he felt no kinship with the earth,
But was inturned upon a course of thoughts,
Dark, wild, and scornful; yet, as sunlight soft
Oft glides o'er earthly shade, his gloom was touched
With passing gleams from a high visioned heaven
Of arm ̈ed knights crusading in the East,

Of grand emprise, and Godfrey of Bouloign
Crowned Christian King, and that fair Princess' face
Sweet looking down the years from marble halls
In old Ferrara ; then he faintly smiled,
And quicker passed and waved the dreams away,
While men bewildered gazed, and sadly said,
" That's Tasso ! "

At Grindelwald, June, 1872.

An Alpine height, Eiger or Mönch,—

Spurning the brawling torrent at its base,

That savage frets in ceaseless earth's turmoil,—

Soars through mid-air, o'er crags and noble woods,

Then bares before the sun green steeps of Alps,

Pine-fringed; still carries upwards scanning eye,

Until, in stainless snow against the blue

Of highest heaven, it wears a gleaming crown

Of sovereign peace, irradiant o'er the land!

All earth's distractions there would seem sublimed

In perfect unity, passion quenched and calmed,

All eager questions hushed, all doubts resolved,—

So near to heaven they've died in heaven's own light.

Yet strange, on that calm top, the searching eye

Oft fearful finds a face in lineament,

Abnormal, vast, mysterious as the years,

A broken image of our human mien,

Upturned to Heaven, as if a soul, o'ercome

In quest too daring, lay unreconciled,

Before all crushing power that feels for nought,—

Smote into silence and a speechless pain,

Under the awful riddle of the world.

On the Scrape.

'TIS early July; there have brooding lain
    Three long white days of rain o'er all the hills;
And now the breaking mists leave bare before
The eager eye vague glimpses of the glens,
Where the moist slatey braes in deep blue gleam,
As if suffused with spreading harebell's hue.
Pure greenery is streaked o'er hill-sides broad
That glen-wards slope, by heather mottled o'er,
Still sombre, yet with pleasing tints of bloom.

At length the rising mists are high upcaught

Within the rest and quiet of the sky,—-

A long low sky of still grey cloud that keeps

A brooding pensive calm, and soft distils

A tender gloom o'er the earth-sea of heights

And glens, that heave and fall far as the line

Of distant Cheviots, whose sheeny tops

Gleam all along the utmost bound of sight,

And hint the presence of the sun above

The moveless cloudy veiling of the hills !

All would be stillness, while the fresh heights feel

Pervading joy in pure life-moisture drunk

From the full bounteous heaven, but snow - white
     sheep

Late shorn, and dotting all green spots of braes,

To one another bleat upon the air;

And burns, that eager filled their urnlike pools

In trouble of the storm, o'erflowing rush

Adown the glens, the joyous messengers

Of sound that fell from the now silent sky!

And curious tiny flowers, that 'neath the storm

Had low in quiet bent, now raise their heads

With uncomplaining looks,—star-wort, pale eyed

And peaceful in its tears, and myriad flowers

Of yellow tormentil, rock-rose that loves

The heights, and mountain speedwell delicate,

Blue cupped milk-wort that ever modest seeks

To lay its peerless face amid the grass;—

Flowerets subdued and gentle, and that ask

No question of the lowering sky, but bow

Submissive to the face of heaven above

Whene'er it darkens into cloudy rain,

And loving rise and bless the sun's return!

The early bracken carefully unbends

Its finger tips inturned, slow feeling for

The sun and balmy air,—a nature where

The blind impulse of life has been subdued,

Or, it would seem, illumed by custom long

Of circling years, and ruling now itself

Through secret sympathy with elements

And powers around,—an inspiration real

As conscious forethought clear, or knowing mind,—

Gleam of the Reason at the root of things!

Around me cluster quaint cloud-berry flowers,

That love the moist slopes of the highest tops,

Pale white, and delicate, and beautiful,

Yet lowly growing 'mid the black peat moss,—

No life with darker root and fairer bloom:

As if the hand of God had secret wrought

Amid the peaty chaos and decay

Of long deep buried years, and from the moss

Entombed, unshaped, unsunned, and colourless,

Set free a form of beauty rare and bright,

To typify the glory and the grace

Which from the dust of death He will awake,

In course of time, on Resurrection morn!

Oh! wot ye not there is a soul in things,

In living form of plant, whence organism

Upsprings, and whence it grows enshaped and ruled,

The lower moulded by the higher power?

Life grounding form, and form sustaining life?

A soul first set within the chaos dull

Of senseless clay, that gathers to itself

The scattered elements of earth and air;

And, vital plastic messenger of God,

In darkness secret works, low 'mid the dust

Of death, until stem, leaf, and flower evolved,

It robes itself to sense in symmetry

Of form, in radiant life and bloom; and, thus,

A mere dim potence moving steadily

Towards its finished bound, arises clear

A perfect thing, in face of heaven and God,

N

With consciousness of destiny fulfilled,

And sympathetic sense of that great life

To which it owes the glory of its own !

'Twas a grand dream of mediæval art,

That from the ashes of the flower consumed

A secret skill might rear the perished form,

And shapeless death might gain the look of life.

God's alchemy is more than art e'er dreamed,

For from the dull chaotic mass of clay,

From out the very dust of hopeless death,

It ever brings us not mere image, fair,

But bright reality of radiant life !

No human sense is here, by day or night,

To lend a conscious form to sight or sound,

And thus redeem from void and vacancy

The vague indefinite of outward things,

And set it high illumed and glorified,

As wondrous pageant process of the world!

For sense alone, and for the sense of man,

Was all this set? This grace of upland form,

This beauty rare, and lonely loveliness;

Gleams roseate that rapid flush o'er knowes,

As radiance dropt from shadeless angel wings,

Bent lovingly o'er this fair earth of ours!

Flowerets that live and bloom, and die upon

The wild; the shadowed pools and rippling turns

Of burns that ceaseless sound by day and night,

At high noon-tide, and 'neath the circling moon.

Must not He, the first of all, be first displayed?

In free fair forms complete within themselves,

That rise and pass, one after one, to fill

The rich life-tide of Time, yet tell that He,

The one abiding Life, is the last ground

Of all the varied show, whose primal joy

Is efflorescence pure, aye flowing on

In endless process-vision of Himself!

Yet all is open to each heart of man
That wills to seek the vision pure, and rise
To love of love, of purity, and truth,
As things sufficient in themselves, thus grow
Into the gracious way of God, and pass
To bloom of life that stirs each eye and heart
By type as winsome as the moorland flower
That ne'er obtrudes its strength of beauty free!

May we whose lot it is to frame ourselves
By motions of free-will, transcendent power,
But reach the rest of nature's silent growths,
In consent perfect with the will of God!
Theirs a spontaneous harmony evolved;
A victory ours, and ever growing, gained
By conquest of ourselves; the scattered parts
Of our whole being gathered into one;

Desire, impulse, and passion led by Will

In tribute, till from lowly grave of thoughts,

The primal elements of our true selves,

There springs the perfect flower of human life,

The dead past risen, quickened, and sublimed !

Among the Hills! Away!

FAR along the empurpled heights,
  Where dews have wreathed the green,
The mists transfigured pass, sun-smit,
  In folds of radiant sheen.
The north-west wind is up in might,
  With clouds for speeding wings;
His gentle bride, the blue clear morn,
  High o'er the hills he brings.
Lo! strength and beauty rare are wed,
  Wed in the sky to-day;
There's hurrying joy in heaven o'erhead;
  Among the hills! Away!

High on the moors the sportive wind

  Kisses the blooming heath;

He plays with the harebell's graceful form,

  Steals the thyme's fragrant breath!

He speeds in gleam, he glides in shade,

  Joy and grief are at play;

The blue clear morn looks loving on;

  Among the hills! Away!

NOTES AND ILLUSTRATIONS.

Page 4, line 9.

The Wood of Caledon.

The "Coed Celyddon" is repeatedly mentioned in the Welsh Bardic remains of the sixth and seventh centuries. It occurs especially in the poems attributed to Myrdin, or Merlin, and in those in which he appears as a speaker.* The centre of the *Coed Celyddon,* or *Nemus Caledonis,* was probably what is now called Tweedsmuir, part of which is known as Tweed Shaws. The wood itself appears to have stretched across the hills to the south, embracing the glens of Meggat, or Rodono, Yarrow, and Ettrick. On the north it extended to the Pentlands, across the Moss of Maw. Westwards it stretched to Godeu, now Cadzow. The districts of Ettrick and Yarrow came afterwards to be known exclusively by the name of "The Forest," though this was much later than is commonly supposed. Falkirk is spoken of in the thirteenth

* See Mr. Skene's admirable edition of *The Four Ancient Books of Wales,* I, 368 ; II, 3, *et alibi.*

century as in " The Forest ;" and in Bruce's time " the
Watyr of Lyne," which joins the Tweed three miles above
Peebles, is apparently regarded by Barbour as part of
" The Forest " :—

> " In all this tyme James of Douglas
> In the forest trawaland was ;
>
> *   *   *   *   *   *
>
> Intill that tyme, him fell throu cass,
> On ane nicht as he trawaland was,
> And thoucht till haiff resting
> . In ane houss on the Watyr of Lyne." *

In the *Historia Britonum* of Nennius of the seventh
century, the scene of Arthur's seventh battle is said to
have been in this wood, " in Silva Caledonis, id est, Cat
Coit Celyddon." There seems to be good ground for sup-
posing that the historical Arthur was the leader, the
Guledig or *Dux Bellorum*, of the Britons who sought to
recover from Saxon, Scot, and Pict their original posses-
sions in the South and West of Scotland—Y Gogled—the
North—as far as to the Firth of Forth, or Scottish Sea. I
have also little doubt but that this seventh battle of Arthur
was fought at Catmore, that is, *the great fight*, now Cademuir, a wavy hill lying a little to the south of the Tweed,
about two miles above the town of Peebles. The four
tops of the ridge still show numerous interesting remains
of the pre-historic dwellings and fortifications with which
they were once crowned ; and there is a space on one of
the summits crowded and solemn with ancient grave-
stones. The eighth Arthurian battle was fought in the

* *The Bruce*, Book VII, l. 213, 221-225.

Gwenstrath, or *White Strath,* in Gala Water, across the hills from Cademuir. The Saxons called the spot Wedale,—dale of woe,—from the disaster they met with there.

It was into the Wood of Caledon that Myrdin, or Merlin, the Welsh Bard, prophet, and enchanter, is said to have fled after the decisive battle of Arderydd in 573. Here too he is reported to have met Kentigern—St. Mungo—the young and ardent apostle of Christianity. Kentigern has left several memorials of himself on the banks of the Tweed. The ancient Church of Stobo—an *ecclesia plebania,* or mother-church—was dedicated to him; and we have, or had, St. Mungo's Well on the slopes of Venlaw.

P. 10, l. 2.

That morn he rode by Ericstane.

Sir James Douglas, known as the good Lord James, after the death of his father in Edward's prison at Berwick, by poison or of a broken heart, set out from St. Andrews to join the party of Robert Bruce. He met Bruce and his friends at Ericstane, near the head of Annandale, on their way to Scone, and there did homage to him as his "rychtwiss King":—

> " . . . . A litill frae Arylkstane
> The Bruce with a great rout he met,
> That raid to Scone for to be set
> In King's stole, and to be King."*

* *The Bruce,* B. II, l. 148.

P. 12, l. 3, 8.

Fruid.   Hawkshaw.

Fruid was a very early property of the Frasers, and remained in the name and collateral line until at least the middle of the sixteenth century.   See prefatory note to *The Lady Fleming's Dream,* p. 137.

Hawkshaw was long the seat of the old family of Porteous—a name which frequently occurs in the feuds of Upper Tweeddale.   This old stock is not without representatives in our time.   Walter Scott, tenth of Thirlestane, originally of Howpaisley, near the head of the Teviot, married Marion, daughter of Sir Patrick Porteous of Hawkshaw. Their son, Patrick Scott, married a daughter of Sir John Murray of Blackbarony.   This Patrick Scott was the direct ancestor of the present Lord Napier and Ettrick.

P. 18, l. 9.

Powmood.

Powmood, or Polmood, was for a very long period the seat of the Hunters.   Their fabulously ancient charter shows the popular impression of their great antiquity. The name is a very early one.   Gulielmus Venator is a witness in the charter of the erection of the Bishopric of Glasgow, by David, Prince of Cumberland, afterwards David I. (1124-1158).   In a charter of Alexander II. (1214-1249) of the lands of Manners (Manor) to William Baddeby, upon the resignation of them by Nicol Corbat, the lands of Norman Hunter are exempted, as the charter bears, " Quas Nicolaus Corbat nobis reddidit, excepta terra quondam Normani Venatoris, quam Malcolumus frater regis Willelmi, ei didit."* This shows that the Hunters had lands in Manor, not far from Polmood, as early as the time of Malcolm IV. (1153-1165). The legend of the death of Bertha, at Powmood, through the jealousy of the Queen of Grimus, is one of our oldest Scottish traditions. There can be no doubt that the most of the properties in Upper Tweeddale were held from the crown as part of the original forest lands, and for services to be rendered to the Scottish monarchs, who came so frequently to enjoy the chace in the district, down to the time of Mary and her son, James VI. Names, traditions, extant charters, all point to this conclusion.

P. 18, l. 13.

Stanhope.

Early in the sixteenth century, William, second son of John Murray of Falahill and Philiphaugh—probably the outlaw Murray of the ballad — acquired the estate of Romanno by his marriage with Janet, only child of William Romanno of that Ilk. Their descendant, Sir David Murray, acquired Stanhope in the time of Charles I. His eldest son was made a baronet by Charles II. in 1664. The daughter of the honoured and gifted Lady Grizzel Baillie married the last laird of Stanhope. Murray of Stanhope had to part with the estates owing to

---

* Nisbet's *Heraldry*, I, 332.

his share in the rising of 1745. They passed altogether from the Murrays in 1769. A great part of the beauty of the Tweed, as it passes through what was the old estate of Hillhouse—now Stobo—is due to the careful planting of forest trees and hedgerows, after a southern fashion, by the last laird of Stanhope, Sir Alexander Murray, from about 1732.

P. 18, l. 15.

Drummelzier.

Drummelzier was originally *Dunmeller,* which would be *Hill of Meller* or *Meldred,* or it may be *Druim Meldred, i.e., Ridge of Meldred,* as in *Drumalbain, Druim Alban.* Either etymology suits the local appearance. Both name and estate are very ancient. The earliest historical notice of its possessors shows it to have been in the hands of the Frasers of Oliver Castle, or a branch of the family : and it continued in the name and family after the death of Sir Simon in 1306. Laurentius Fraser, or Frisel, was laird of Drummelzier in the thirteenth century. He was alive in 1261. He also possessed the lands of Makerston. His son, Laurence de Frisle, is on Ragman Roll of 1296. His eldest daughter seems to have married a Tweedie, and brought as her dowrie the estate of Drummelzier ; while the second daughter married Dougal Macdougal, and brought with her the estate of Makerston, in the reign of David II. (1329-1370).* This was the origin, apparently, of the brave, restless, turbulent, and red-

* Anderson's *Historical Account of the Family of Fraser,* p. 6.

handed stock of the Tweedies, whose motto, "*Thole and think*," proved so ludicrously in contrast with their character. "Thole," *i. e.*, suffer patiently, they never did ; and "thinking" seems to have been as little in their line. At the same time, I do not suppose that they were much, if anything, worse than a good many of their neighbours.

P. 19, l. 15.

Lord Fleming's dying wail.

See prefatory note to *The Lady Fleming's Dream*, p. 165.

P. 20, l. 6 ; p. 21, l. 3.

The Logan Lee.   Mossfennan Yett.

> " The King rode round the Merecleugh Head,
> Wi' spotted hounds and spaniels three,
> Then lichted doon at Mossfennan Yett,
> A little below the Logan Lee."

Other version :—

> " The King rode round the Merecleugh Head,
> Booted and spurred as we a' did see,
> Syne dined wi' a lass at Mossfennan Yett,
> A little below the Logan Lee."

These are fragments of a very old ballad.   Possibly the following stanza is part of it :—

> "Some say I lo'e young Powmood,
> Some say he lo'es nae me,
> But I wot I'm a match for the best o' his blood,
> Though I hadna a ewe on the Logan Lee."

We are indebted to Miss J. M. Watson for several frag-
mentary stanzas of this ancient ballad.*

Mossfennan is an old estate in Tweeddale. William
Purvoys de Mosspennach gave a charter about 1214, the
end of the reign of William the Lion, granting to the
monks of Melrose a free passage through his lands to
their property of Kingledoors.† Mossfennan was held
for some generations by a family of Scots — of whom
was the heiress referred to in the text. This estate,
along with some adjoining lands, was erected in 1538
into one of the five baronies possessed by Malcolm, the
third and powerful Lord Fleming, and son of the Lord
John, murdered by the Tweedies. It has been in the
possession of the family of the present proprietor, the
Rev. William Welsh, for more than a hundred and fifty
years.

P. 22, l. 10.

Ancient Dawyck.

Dawyck is one of the oldest estates and homesteads
in Tweeddale, or in the south of Scotland. For more
than four hundred years — from before 1296 to 1704
—it was the principal residence and property of the
line of Veitch of Dawyck—a family distinguished for
the number of its sons who fought and fell on home
and foreign battle-fields, during the middle ages and
down to near our own time. Nor was the name unknown

---

* See her finely touched and interesting *Life in Our Village.*
† Nisbet's *Heraldry*, I, xviii, p. 213.

in law and statesmanship. The family gave a President to the Parliament of Paris, and a leading statesman to the Scottish Parliament of the seventeenth century. There is historical evidence of the name on Tweedside as far back as the time of Alexander II. (1214-1249). In his reign, at the Court of Roxburgh, we find Alexander la Uache as witness to an ecclesiastical deed.* Before 1296, the family had obtained Dauwic, or Dawyck. William le Vache is on the Ragman Roll of that year. Along with Dawyck, the Veitches held, either in the person of their head or through collateral branches, other estates in Peeblesshire, particularly Earlshaugh, Glenbreck, Kingside, Hallmanor, Glenrath, Castlehill, Woodhouse, and The Glen. In Selkirkshire they held North Sinton, acquired in 1407 by gift from Archibald, the fourth Earl of Douglas, to his friend and armourbearer, the knightly laird of Dawyck, who fell with him at Verneuil in 1424. The estates of the family became mortgaged in the time of Sir John Veitch, Commissioner of Works under Charles I., and for long a prominent member of the Scottish Parliament. Sir John disinterestedly spent the greater part of his patrimony on the repairs of public works in Scotland—especially Holyrood and its chapel—during the troubles of his time. For money or skill expended he received neither compensation nor thanks from the Government either of the Restoration or Revolution. Sir John Veitch had married in 1643, or perhaps earlier,

* *Registrum Episcopatus Glasguensis*, p. 126.

O

Christian, daughter of James Naesmyth of Posso.* Their son, John Veitch, held Dawyck until 1704, when he sold the mortgaged estates to his cousin, James Naesmyth of Posso, who was made a baronet of Nova Scotia in 1706. Sir John Murray Naesmyth of Posso is the direct lineal representative of the first baronet of Posso, and thus, through the female line, a descendant of the old house of Dawyck. The motto of the Veitches is *Famam extendimus factis;* the crest a cow's head, with three cows' heads, sable, on a silver shield. The motto of the Naesmyths is *Non arte sed marte*—the arms show the crossed and broken hammers on the shield.

P. 24, l. 15.

Sainted Gordian.

The ancient Church of Manor, which stood near the spot where the Newholmhope Burn joins the Manor, on the estate of Posso, was dedicated either to Saint Gordian or to Saint Gorgon—most probably the former. It was known as St. Gordian's Kirk or St. Gorgham's Chapel, and was entire until near the middle of the seventeenth century. St. Gordian, according to the common account, was beheaded at Rome under Julian the Apostate, about the year 362. His feast was kept by the Scottish Church on the 10th of May.† For long the place where the ancient church stood was only indicated by the green

---

* *Posso Papers.*

† Bishop Forbes' *Kalendar of Scottish Saints,* p. 357.

mounds that cover its ruins. Sir John Murray Naesmyth of Posso, with loving care, has recently set up a simple and touching cross of stone to mark the site of the ancient house of prayer, and the place of sepulture, for many hundreds of years, of those who dwelt in peel and cot in the secluded valley of Manor—"in reductâ valle Manoris." Those in the district who have any sense of historic reverence will from the heart thank the Laird of Posso for his own heart-prompted memorial of days and lives long gone, yet worthy of our remembrance and our quiet thought.

P. 39, l. 18.

Roxburgh's smooth green mounds.

The Castle of Roxburgh was a principal seat of Scottish royalty, in the comparatively peaceful and prosperous period of the monarchy that preceded the War of Independence. It then formed nearly the centre of the Lowland Kingdom, for Cumbria, extending far into the north of England, was an appanage of the second son of the Scottish king. As late as about the year 1116, when David, afterwards David I., was Prince of Cumbria, it is described as a district lying between England and Scotland : " Regione quadam inter Angliam et Scotiam sita."[*] After the War of Independence, the possession of the Castle formed a nearly constant subject of struggle be-

[*] *Inquisitio per Dauid Principem Cumbrensem de terris ecclesie Glasguensi pertinentibus facta—Registrum Episcopatus Glasguensis,* p. 5.

tween English and Scotch. It was in an attempt to recover it that James II. met his death.

P. 48, l. 19 : p. 49, l. 1.

. . . . . . *Or slanting beams,*
Through watery air, lie 'red upon the rain.'

> "The boy has buckled his belt about,
>   And through the greenwood ran ;
> And he came to the lady's bower,
>   Before the day did dawn.
>
> "O sleep ye, wake ye, Lillie Flower?
>   *The red sun's on the rain :*
> Ye're bidden come to Silverwood,
>   But I doubt ye'll never win hame."
>
> *Jellon Grame.*[*]

P. 54, l. 2-4.

The wodewale like a bell the forest through ;
And to his ear the mavis mellow-sweet
Aye turned to soft complaining in her song.

> "I herde the jaye, and the 'throstelle,'
> The mawys menyde of hir songe,
> The wodewale beryde als a belle,
> That all the wode about me ronge."

The wodewale is said to be the wood-lark, or wood-pecker, the *oriol* of the early romances—

> "Plus est delit en le oriol
> Escoter la note de l'*oriol*."[†]

[*] Child's *Ballads*, II, 287.

[†] Quoted by Wedgwood, *Dictionary of English Etymology, sub voce Oriel.*

The oldest English version of the Ballad of Thomas the Rhymer, from which this stanza is taken, proceeds :

"Allone in longynge, thus als I lay,
  Undre nethe a semeley trie,
  'Saw I' whare a lady gaye
  'Came ridand' ouer a longe lee.

   *   *   *   *   *   *   *

  Hir palfraye was a dappill gray ;
  Swilke one I saghe me never none :
  Als dose the soune, on someres day,
  That fair lady hir selfe scho shone.

   *   *   *   *   *   *   *

  Thomas rathely up he rase,
  And he rane ouer that mountayne hye ;

   *   *   *   *   *   *   *

  She ledde him in at Eldon hill,
  Undir nethe a derne lee ;
  Where it was dirk as mydnyght mirk,
  And ever the water till his knee.
  The montenans of dayes three,
  He herd bot swoghyne of the flode ;
  At the laste, he sagde 'full wa es mee !
  Almaste I dye, for fawte of fude.'
  She broghte him agayne to Eldon trie,
  Undir nethe that greenwood spraye ;
  In Huntlee bannkes es merry to bee,
  Where fowles synges bothe nyght and daye,
  Iferre owtt in yon mountain graye,
  Thomas, my fawkon byggis a neste ;
  A fawcoun is an eglis praye ;
  Fforthi in na place may he reste.
  Ffare well, Thomas ; I wend my waye ;
  Ffor me behouys thir benttis brown."

               Thomas the Rhymer.*

    * Child's *Ballads*, I, 97.

These verses have an unmistakeable air of antiquity, and a charm wholly inexpressible. The poem, moreover, like the earliest of the *Robin Hood* ballads, shows a pure feeling for nature, which died out alike of Scottish and English poetry for several centuries afterwards. Some of the lines in these old ballads have a realism which strikes one with the power of the first fresh visiting by Nature of the human heart. In a later version, the ride to Fairyland of the Queen and Thomas is given with certain accessory features which do not derogate from its Homeric power :—

> "O they rade on, and farther on,
>   And they waded through rivers aboon the knee,
> And they saw neither sun nor mune,
>   But they heard the roaring of the sea.

> "It was mirk, mirk night, and there was nae stern light,
>   And they waded through red blude to the knee ;
> For a' the blude that's shed on earth
>   Rins through the springs o' that countrie."

That Thomas the Rhymer was a person who lived by the Leader, and during the greater part of the thirteenth century, I see no ground for doubting.

P. 59, l. 12, to p. 60, l. 15.

See *Burd Ellen* in Child's *Ballads*, and the very curious legend there given—(Vol. I., p. 245 *et seq.*) The legend has suggested some of the physical, or rather hyperphysical features in those lines.

˙P. 66, l. 14.

Ossian.

One of the oldest of the Ossianic poems, entitled *Cal-*
hon and Colvala, refers to the Tweed in some part of
its upper reaches. There is a probability, both from local
situation and on other grounds, that the Alt-Teutha, or
Fort of Tweed referred to in the poem, was what is
now called Tinnies' Castle, near Drummelzier, and at the
opening of the old highway down the Strath of Biggar
Water to the Tweed.*

P. 70, l. 8.

Neidpath's old grey tower.

This ancient fortress stands in one of the boldest and
most picturesque reaches of the Tweed, a little more than
a mile above the town of Peebles. It was the principal
residence in the seventeenth century of John Hay, ninth
Lord Yester, second Earl, and first Marquis of Tweeddale
—a direct descendant of Hay of Lochquharret, and Mary,
the daughter of Sir Simon Fraser. Lord Tweeddale took
a very prominent part in the public events of the times of
Charles I., the Commonwealth, the Restoration, and the
Revolution. He died in 1697. To him is currently
attributed the beautiful song of " Tweedside "—the earliest
piece of poetry inspired by the Tweed which has come
down to us :—

> "When Maggie and me were acquaint,
> I carried my noddle fu' high,

* For the poem see Clark's *Ossian*, Vol. I, p. 315.

Nae lintwhite in a' the gay plain,
Nae gowdspink sae bonny as she !

"I whistled, I piped, and I sang,
I wooed but I cam' nae great speed,
Therefore I maun wander abroad,
And lay my banes far frae the Tweed.

"To Maggie my love I did tell,
My tears did my passion express ;
Alas ! for I lo'ed her ower weel,
And the women lo'e sic a man less !

"Her heart it was frozen and cauld ;
Her pride had my ruin decreed :
Therefore I maun wander abroad,
And lay my banes far frae the Tweed !"

P. 81, l. 7.

By lee light of the moon on southern hills.

Lee is lonesome.

"Sad Willie raise, put on his claise,
Drew till him his hose and shoon,
And he is on to Annie's bower,
By the lee light o' the moon."

*Sweet Willie and Fair Annie.**

P. 84, l. 9-14.

The reader may refer to the grand old ballad of *The Outlaw Murray*, which is animated throughout by the view here given of the tenure in the middle ages of landed property on the Borders :—

"Ettricke Foreste is a feir foreste,
In it grows manie a semelie tree ;

* Child's *Ballads*, II, 138.

There's hart and hynde, and dae and rae,
  And of a' wilde beastes grete plentie.
Their's a feir castelle, bigged wi' lyme and stane :
  O ! gin it stands not pleasauntlie !
In the forefront o' that castelle feir,
  Twa unicorns are bra' to see ;
There's the picture of a knight, and a ladye bright,
  And the grene hollin abune their brie.

  * * * * * *

' The King of Scotlonde sent me here,
  And, gude Outlaw, I am sent to thee ;
I wad wot of whom you hald your landis,
  Or man, wha may thy master be?'
' Thir lands are MINE !' the Outlaw said ;
  ' I ken nae King in Christentie ;
Frae Soudron I this Foreste wan,
  When the King nor his knights were not to see !

  * * * * * *

Thir lands of Ettrick Foreste feir,
  I wan them from the enemie ;
Like as I wan them, sae will I keep them,
  Contrair a' Kingis in Christentie.

  * * * * * *

Feir Philiphaugh is mine by right,
  And Lewinshope still mine shall be ;
Newark, Foulshiels, and Tinnies baith,
  My bow and arrow purchased me.' "

The period of the Outlaw Murray is not later than the early part of the sixteenth century. His surrender of his lands to the king, and the acceptance of the same from him under a feudal investiture, are not without historical probability. The outlaw was apparently John Murray of Falahill and Philiphaugh, in the time of James IV. This monarch, in 1508, gave to John Murray a charter, after resignation, as in the ballad, of half of the lands of

Philiphaugh; and in 1509 added the whole lands of Pitgyl in Selkirkshire, and confirmed to him the sheriff-ship of the county. This heritable office remained in the family of Philiphaugh until the act abolishing all such jurisdictions in 1747. A ballad lamenting the death of the Outlaw at the hand of Buccleuch was long chanted in the forest. It has now unfortunately perished from memory. The same aggressive policy which led the Scotts of Buccleuch to attack the falling Douglases, prompted the murder of Murray, and their secret action against the Laird of Gilnockie, which resulted in his cruel and barely judicial execution. The Philiphaugh family is the oldest stock of the Murrays in the Border Counties, whose claims admit of being tested by public historical documents. There is a charter of the lands of Fala by Lord James Douglas to Roger de Moravia, filius Archibaldi, in 1321, and Archibaldus (Erchebaud) de Moravia is on the Ragman Roll of 1296. The Murrays of Blackbarony claim an old and independent descent. They certainly had Halton or Blackbarony as early as the beginning of the reign of James I. Unfortunately the estate of Black-barony was severed from the title, and from the male representation of the family, by Sir Alexander Murray, the fourth baronet, about the middle of last century.

P. 85, l. 16, 17.

' By deeds we spread our fame.'   ' By might not art,'—.
The mottoes of the time, at length entwined
In one.

See Note at p. 22, l. 10.

P. 99, l. 7, etc.

This Muse would speak in eerie dream o' night.

These lines refer to the famous Battle of Otterbourne between the two Lords Henry and Ralph Percy, and James, second Earl of Douglas—" miles acerrimus et Anglis semper infestissimus." It took place in the beginning of August, 1388 :—

> " It fell about the Lammas tide,
>   When muirmen winn their hay,
> The doughty Douglas boune him to ride,
>   Into England to take a prey."

The dream and death of the Earl are thus referred to :—

> " But I hae dreamed a dreary dream,
>   Beyond the Isle of Sky ;
> I saw a dead man winn a field,
>   And I wot that man was I.
>
> *   *   *   *   *   *
>
> ' My nephew good,' the Douglas said,
>   ' What recks the death of ane !
> Last night I dreamed a dreary dream,
>   And I ken the day's thy ain.
>
> ' My wound is deep ; I fain would sleep ;
>   Take thou the vanguard of the three,
> And hide me by the bracken bush,
>   That grows on yonder lily lee.
>
> ' O bury me by the bracken bush,
>   Beneath the blooming brier,
> Let never living mortal ken
>   That e'er a kindly Scot lies here.' "

P. 102, l. 7.

Dark was that eve when the strong swell of Clyde.

The following verses represent the stage of fear in relation to wild, stern Nature, and the power of will roused by passion to face and overcome it :—

> " He mounted on his coal-black steed,
>   And fast he rode awa' ;
> But, ere he cam to Clyde's Water,
>   Fu' loud the wind did blaw.
> As he rode ower yon high, high hill,
>   And doun yon dowie glen,
> There was a roar in Clyde's Water
>   Wad fear'd a hunder men.
>
> *   *   *   *   *   *
>
> O roaring Clyde, ye roar ower loud,
>   Your streams seem wondrous strang ;
> Mak me your wreck as I come back,
>   But spare me as I gang."
>
>   *Willie and Fair Margaret.**

Has the intensity of the love-passion, or the daring of the human will, been more powerfully expressed than in these simple words?

Other stanzas in the Border Ballads represent the transition stage between the dread of the stern aspects of Nature and the contemplative love of them, which is characteristic of the full development of the poetic sense :—

> " The King was comin' through Caddon ford
>   And full five thousand men was he ;

* Child's *Ballads*, II, 171.

They saw the derke forest them before,
They thought it awesome for to see."

P. 104, l. 6.
Ettrick's fair-haired Shepherd.

The reference is, of course, to James Hogg,—the author of *The Queen's Wake,*—born in 1770, died in 1835. The Shepherd was a man of high and true, though far from artistic, poetic genius. His power of touching the super-sensible, especially the weird and awful, has not been surpassed in our literature. His real position as a poet has been greatly obscured in the popular estimate by the extravagant and one-sided representation of him in the *Noctes Ambrosianæ.* His true place is second only to that of Burns, and he has left pictures of a fanciful grace and beauty which Burns never essayed to paint.

P. 106, l. 16.
Leyden.

John Leyden, the friend and coadjutor of Scott in the collection of the *Minstrelsy of the Borders,* and the author of *The Scenes of Infancy,* died too early for his powers and his fame. Leyden was born at Denholm, in Teviot-dale, in 1775, and he died of fever at Java in 1811, at the premature age of 36. Leyden was a master of rhythm, and there are passages of great vigour, of fine and true feeling, and powerful description, in the too little known *Scenes of Infancy.* Leyden, Hogg, and Scott all drew inspiration from the same sources,—the traditions of the past and the Border scenery around them. They had the courage of their surroundings. There is now a tendency in Scotland to forget our obligations to Leyden and Hogg for the share they had, along with Scott, in introducing into our literature healthy human feeling, the traditions of the past, and the fresh breath of hill and stream. Leyden and Hogg, though drawing from the same source, had their inspiration at first hand, and each has qualities of intellect and imagination which gives him a power peculiarly his own. So far as massive intelligence is concerned, Leyden's promise was greatly higher than Scott's realization.

P. 130, l. 5-10.

See Barbour's graphic picture of the state of the country at this period—*The Bruce*, Bk. I, l. 179-224. Nothing can be more touching than the utter arbitrariness of will depicted in these lines :—

> " And gyff that ony man thaim by
> Had ony thing that was worthy,
> As horse, or hund, or othir thing,
> That was pleasand to their liking ;
> With rycht or wrang it have wald thai.
> And gyff ony wald thai withsay ;
> Thai suld swa do, that thai suld tyne
> Othir land, or lyff, or leyff in pine."

P. 130, l. 15.

Gamyn.

> " When Alysandyr our Kyng was dede,
> That Scotland led in luve and le,

Away was sons of ale and brede,
Of wyne and wax, of gamyn and gle.
Our gold was changyd into lede,
Chryst born into virgynyte,
Succour Scotland and remede,
That stad is in perplexitie." *

P. 139, l. 6, 10.

Greyking. Chevachée.

Greyking is more specific than dawn. It indicates the appearance and fading of the dim grey or half-lit misty sky at the approach of the rising sun. *Chevachée* is originally a military exploit on horseback, by a small body of men. It had no necessary connection, as some suppose, with a predatory purpose. Such an aim came in the middle period of our history particularly to be associated with it; but originally it was simply a military movement with the design of reconnoitring, surprising, or harassing the enemy. The Uhlans in the late Franco-Prussian War were constantly making such exploits. One of the earliest applications of the word we have is in an order addressed by Edward I. to Sir Simon Fraser of Oliver (Nov. 25th, 1298), to aid John de Kingston, English Governor of Edinburgh Castle, in a *chevachée* or raid upon the national party under Buchan and Soulis with twenty armed horses *(chevaus covertz). Chevy-Chace,* though it is commonly supposed to be a corruption of Cheviot Chace, the undoubted scene of the raid, is no doubt merely a popular form of *chevachée.*

* Fragment of song preserved by Wyntoun.

Greyking, fire-flauchts, etc. (p. 156, l. 1), are fine old Teutonic words. I use them on principle. Many others of the same sort would prove a valuable addition to our present vocabulary. They have died out of the existing form of the language, but, if needed, they ought to be restored to use. They are valuable synonymes; they express with precision real appearances to sense, which we have no words fitted accurately to denote; and they are rhetorically advantageous. Every synonyme which indicates a new aspect of an object is an addition to the expressiveness of a language; it also adds to its power and variety as a means of impression.

P. 139, l. 11.

Horsbroc.

This is perhaps the oldest surviving name still in possession of lands in Peeblesshire, of which we have record. Simon de Horsbroc is mentioned in the Chronicle of the Abbey of Melrose, as early as between 1214 and 1249, that is, during the reign of Alexander II. A Simon de Horsbroc is a constant associate in arms of Sir Simon Fraser of Oliver towards the end of the same century. They were both taken prisoners at Dunbar, were together under Edward at Flanders, and both received back their estates from the English king at the same time. Horsbroc, the friend of Simon Fraser, was probably the son of the Simon de Horsbroc mentioned in the Melrose records. Sir Simon Fraser, *pater*, as he is called in the old deeds, died in 1291. The towers of Horsbroc and Neidpath were in the line of communication along the Tweed, and flashed constantly to each other the warning of the beacon-fire. It is very probable that young Simon Fraser and young Horsbroc knew each other as lads on Tweedside, ere they set out to earn the laurel of knighthood together. The old name is now changed to that of Horsbrugh, and some of the ancient lands, forfeited and restored in the thirteenth century, remain with the descendants of Simon de Horsbroc.

P. 139, l. 13.

Burnet.

Burnet was originally of Burnet Ville, supposed to be Burnetland, near Broughton. A *Robertus Burnet de Burnetvilla* is mentioned as early as the time of the charter of foundation of the Abbey of Selkirk by Earl David, youngest son of Malcolm Canmore. This must have been before 1124—the accession of David to the throne. The Burnets held the estate of Barns, often conjoining with it other lands in Manor Water, for upwards of seven hundred years. The estate of Barns passed from this ancient family in 1836. The line is now represented by William Burnett, Esq.

P. 140, l. 1.

Posso's Laird.

The family of Baird, originally Barde, le Barde, held Posso for many generations. The *Boar passant* on their shield indicates the view taken of the origin of the name, but the surmise that *Baird* is originally Barde or Minstrel is quite as probable. Gordon, Nisbet, Swinton, Ridpath, carry boar's heads. It was naturally a common cognizance, The name of Baird had a much earlier place in Peeblesshire than is generally supposed. *Thomas de Burdis*, no doubt *Bardis*, was Sheriff of Peebles in 1296, when he received Edward's instructions to restore their lands to those lairds who had sworn fealty to him. The name occurs several times on the Ragman Roll. About 1541, Michael Naesmyth, of the Royal Household, and Chamberlain to the Archbishop of St. Andrews, married Elizabeth Baird, co-heiress of John Baird of Posso. Her grandfather, Sir Gilbert, had fallen at Flodden in 1513. The Posso estate thus passed to the Naesmyths, who represent the line of the Bairds of Posso. The famous eyrie of "Posso Crag" is on the estate; and James Naesmyth of Posso, a man of note in his time, was Falconer to James VI.

P. 143, l. 6.

Bole.

Bole is a narrow opening or window in old buildings for air and light.

P. 144, l. 3.

Frusch.

An old onomatopoetic word, indicating the grinding or friction sound of breakage, especially of wood.

P. 155, l. 16.

Fee.

Fee is deer, or stag — a common word in the old ballads.

P. 155, l. 17.

Raches.

Raches are deerhounds.

P. 156, l. 8.

Stour.

Stour is troubled motion, hence applied to dust-storm and battle.

P. 157, l. 6.

Dreva's Laird.

The small estate of Dreva was for long an appanage of the Tweedies of Drummelzier. It was held usually by a younger son, and then probably by a cadet of the family. The Tweedies of Dreva do not appear to have been an improvement on the parent breed. At the Justice Aire of Edinburgh, 1502-3, 4th February, John Tweedy of Drummelzier, Walter Tweedy in Hawmyris, and William Tweedy there, became surety for entry of Gilbert Tweedy [of Dreva] for slaughter of Edward Huntair of Polmude. Some thirty-three years later, January 26th, 1565-6, Adame Tweedy of Dravey was "delatit of the cutting of Robert

Rammage's lugges, and demembering of him thereof."
He pleaded the King and Queen's remission of November
30th, 1565—the "date of remission of the gudman of
Drawayis." Nothing was done to him ; William Tweedy
of Drummelzier became, according to the usual formula,
surety to satisfy parties.*

P. 157, l. 14.

They blew the mort on the Wormhill Head.

The *mort* was the notes blown on the horn at the death
of the deer.

> " They hunted high, they hunted low,
>   By heathery hill and birken shaw ;
> They raised a buck on Rooken edge,
>   And blew the mort at fair Ealylawe."
>   *The Death of Parcy Reed.*

* Pitcairn's *Criminal Trials*, I, * 474-5.

GLASGOW:
PRINTED AT THE UNIVERSITY PRESS.

www.ingramcontent.com/pod-product-compliance
Lightning Source LLC
Chambersburg PA
CBHW030103030726
47498CB00007B/2233